AN EXTRAORDINARY
TURN OF EVENTS

Also by J.C. Hopkins

NOVELS

The Perfect Fourth
All of This
I Was a Teenage Communist

POETRY

New York City Love Story
2020 is Hindsight
October to October
Summer of Blue Humidity
From Far Rockaway to Windsor Terrace

AN EXTRAORDINARY TURN OF EVENTS

an anti dystopian novel by

J.C. Hopkins

EPONYMOUS BOOKS

Published by Eponymous Books
eponymousbooks.com

ISBN: 979-8-9915091-3-8
First Edition
Cover Design by Carter Gill

"Apples fall from trees to sow other apples which also fall from trees in the hope that these apples will become stars like the sun which makes apples grow." - Picabia

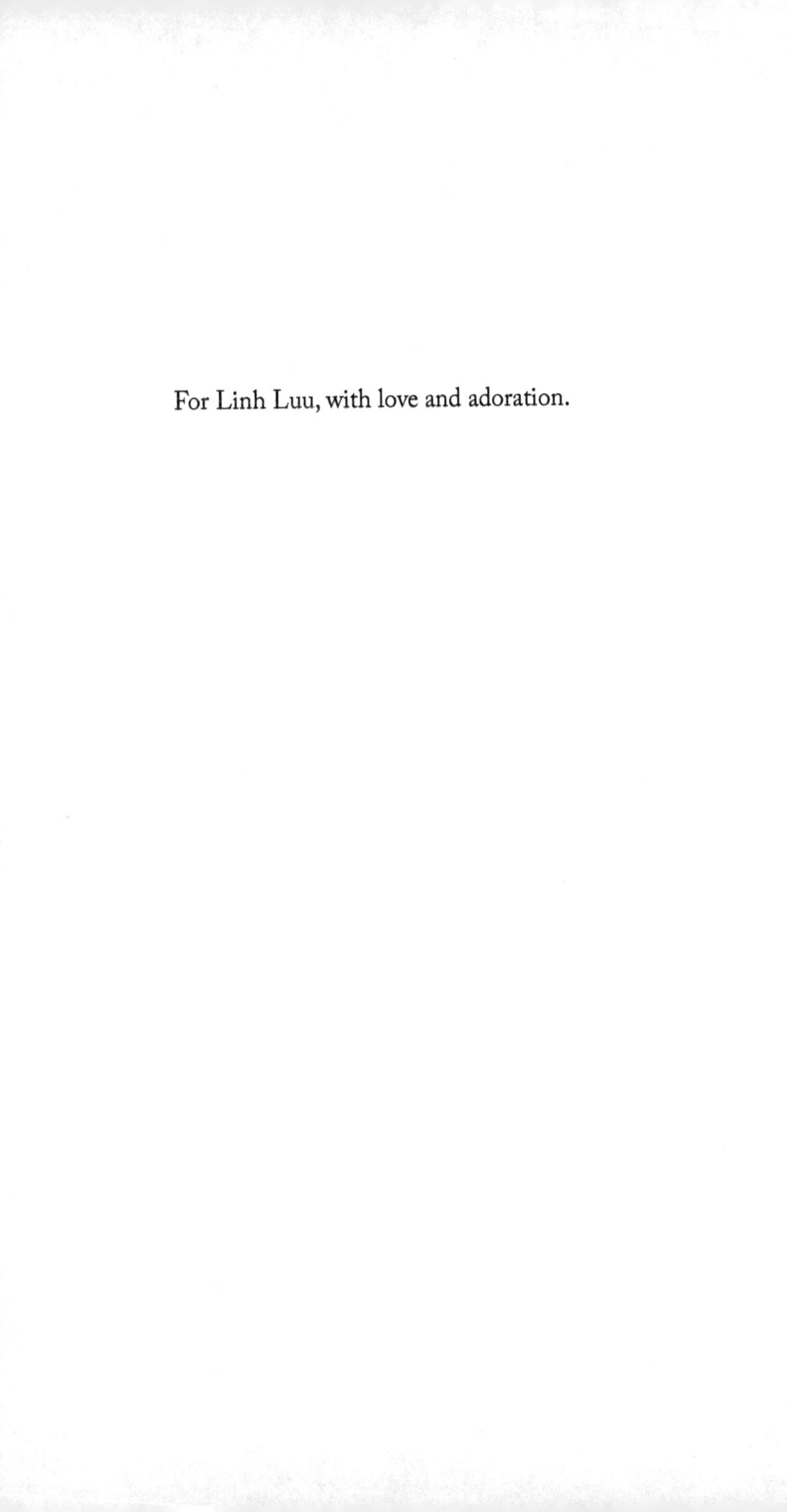

For Linh Luu, with love and adoration.

PART ONE

CHAPTER 1

◆

I am dead. I am so dead.

I am dead because I died. I died and so I am dead.

The EKG pulsed slower and slower, arrhythmic; like someone on Quaaludes tapping out goodbye in Morse code. And then there was just one long tone.

They unplugged all of what had been plugged into me and left the room. And I was still dead. I don't know for how long. I don't know because, for me, time snapped.

Many years later . . .

I entered Café Luxembourg wearing a black bespoke suit. The hostess greeted me with a wan smile, though belabored it was genuine; I was a regular. She wore a beige trench coat buttoned up to the neck. "Freakin' cold tonight, don't know why we have to keep the door open." She sat me in the front part of the restaurant, next to a woman apparently also dining alone. The hostess handed me a menu, smiled, this time wryly and walked away. I took a brief glance at the woman seated to my left. Her unjaded demeanor emanated from a perfectly poised posture. Her dark hair was cut in a shag. She wore a viridian cashmere cardigan over a black V-neck dress and a string of small pearls hung elegantly from around a neck worthy of Modigliani. Behind black vintage cat eye frames were dark brown eyes that blinked alluringly in my direction; she was nerdy coquette. I am alone and at times lonely, yet not lonely enough that I can be tempted, if not tempted, motivated to approach a woman no matter how felicitous. I have taken a vow to only consort with the city: New York City. Finally, I have some means and am putting it to good use. Spending it in fine restaurants, theater, and hearing music at the various concert halls around town. And going to the opera. Alone. Tonight, to the Metropolitan Opera House; a new opera, recently commissioned and completed, with a libretto by Sarah Ruhl and music composed by Matthew Aucoin. It tells the story of Orpheus and Eurydice—only unlike the many previous realizations, this opera tells the story from Eurydice's point of view. Or so I had read in *The New Yorker*.

I looked over the menu and decided on the kale Caesar and the brook trout. The waitress came over and I gave her my order. The woman next to me ordered the exact same thing. I took out my little red notebook and started making notes for the novel I was about to start writing. And, as if it were inevitable, as if it were always meant to happen this way, the woman spoke to me. "Are you a writer?" I put down my pen and turned toward her. She looked at me expectantly. I told her, "In fact I am, or was purported to be." She laughed. "As Georges Perec said, 'I wanted to write and I've written. By dint of writing, I've become a writer. For myself alone first of all, and for a long time and today for others.'" I had memorized the Perec not because I was waiting to say it to someone, not to impress a woman, I memorized it because I liked it. Nevertheless, I felt like an ass for reciting it like a two-bit method actor.

I explained that I was working on a novel about a burp fetishist and her eccentric clientele, one of whom stiffs her, so she kills him. It was just an idea and probably wouldn't go anywhere, yet I found it amusing; and so did she as I told it to her. She had a lilting laugh. I discovered later that when she is uninhibited, when she is particularly amused, it can be more of a full, guttural laugh; her eyes alight, and she is powerless over the action of laughing, which seizes her entire body, a cathartic kind of laugh, very enjoyable to behold. She asked my name, and I tell her that it is Geronimo Vang. "That's my last name, too!" she said, barely controlling her amazement at this uncanny coincidence. At this point in time, it is what my name is. It's what my passport says, anyway.

I looked at my watch. Almost seven. The opera was to begin at 7:30. The waitress came over and asked if I would like dessert. I turned to the woman and suggested the idea of sharing a dessert. I am not sure why I did this since I was in a bit of a rush, and again, she is this other person, and it goes against my vow of aloneness; yet there was something about her. She was attractive in a way that set her apart. In other words, her attractiveness transcends societal constructs, because it is unique, only her own, unlike anyone's I had ever encountered. I found out later that, depending on light and angle, the shape and contours of her face take on an almost unlimited variety of looks; as if she were a model for a thousand different portraitists. And yet she is young, younger than me. I am not sure how much younger, because I don't really know how old I am. That is because of all those years I spent in the wild.

Because we sat side by side, I could not take in the full spectrum of her face, and turning toward her was an awkward contortion. So, I had to rely on my senses. Which is what I have come to rely on ever since I died. Sense and intuition. How long to stay somewhere and when to leave. It has kept me in motion and has kept me surviving and now prospering. My intuition says to keep away, to not get too close to anyone. Not that I haven't slept, or if not slept, had sex with women in all of these ensuing years since I died. A few unremarkable times. But I am alone. Fundamentally alone, and I like it that way. Or thought I liked it that way. She reached for her water glass and touched my elbow, and all of the skin in that region began to tingle. Not static electricity. Not that, another phenomenon. I asked her name, and she told me, Minh. Minh Vang.

I told her about a movie that I had just seen, a film called *Licorice Pizza*. And how this film, in many ways, mirrored, at least on the surface of it, the novel that I had recently written and that had been published by one of the big five. My novel sold moderately and was picked up by a streaming platform to be made into a miniseries. Both the film *Licorice Pizza* and my novel take place in the 1970s in Southern California. The film is a lighthearted love story, and mine is more of a bildungsroman murder mystery. I devised the plot and the setting completely from my imagination; from looking at photographs of Stephen Shore's and reading Roberto Bolaño and Raymond Chandler.

"Yes, I would like to see *Licorice Pizza* with you," she said.

"Oh, that's great. May I have your number?"

She told me her number which I scrawled on the front page of my notebook.

"Are you going to be able to read that?"

"Yes. I think so. Now. What will we have for dessert?"

She looked at the dessert menu and said resolutely, "The banana mousse."

And even though it did not sound particularly tantalizing to me, the way she said banana did, as if each syllable were a word.

We chatted a little more while eating the mousse. I, taking small spoonfuls, and she more vigorously digging in. She told me that she was finishing her MFA at Columbia for literary fiction.

"Where did *you* go to college?" she asked.

"The streets, baby, the streets," I said facetiously.

She released a muffled laugh, furrowed her brows, and said, "That's where I wish to study. The streets. Yet, since I got a full scholarship, and Columbia pays for me to be here, and New York is where I want to be . . . case closed. I love Vietnam, which is where I am from, although I have been in the U.S. since I was fifteen. I just feel intrinsically drawn to this city. It's the old MFA versus NYC debate. The MFA wins the debate by default because of my visa needs. Still, I envy you."

"What's the old MFA versus NYC debate about?"

"I think it was an argument originally found in a David Foster Wallace essay entitled 'The Fictional Future.' That teachers in the MFA program would much rather be writing than teaching, and therefore resent their students who in turn churn out boring, technically proficient workshop stories. And that one could learn more about writing by living and by reading what inspires them."

"Do you feel that way?"

"Sometimes."

"Well, I think you are lucky to be at Columbia, and no doubt talented."

"Why do you say that?"

"Just a feeling."

I was compelled to confide in her. In a manner unlike I had ever confided in anyone. To tell her my whole story. Even though by revealing my darkest secrets I could potentially be putting everything at stake. It was bad enough that I had written the novel. My publisher told me that I would have to go on a book tour and answer questions from the press about who I am, or who Geronimo Vang is. But there is not much to go on. Born in Vietnam and died anonymously in San Francisco at the age of fifty-two. And now he is me, since I purchased his identity. He never died. And I never went on a book tour.

On the way to the Met, I Googled Minh on my new iPhone — Minh Vang — and yes indeed, she was in the fiction MFA program at Columbia. A novelist. In a brief interview she gave to the *Columbia Journal*, she is quoted as saying that her idea of writing is not to be chained to the chair; it is to go out and live life and seek new experiences. I guess I am a new experience, though I feel that there is something more to it. There is a bigger reason why we had been seated together, why we were curious to know one another. This curiosity is new to me, and perhaps a dangerous turn.

I enjoyed the opera, *Eurydice*, with its contemporary setting and concise storytelling. I was especially moved by the moment when the father, a stentorian baritone singing a devastating aria, goes into the river of forgetfulness and obliterates his memory. The river of forgetfulness where the dead pass through, losing their memories and even language.

CHAPTER 2

◆

We made plans to meet at Veselka, a Ukrainian restaurant in the East Village. When I got there I found that there was not a two-top available for at least thirty minutes. We would miss the movie. I texted Minh to meet me at B&H Dairy just across Second Avenue. She texted back a thumbs-up emoji. B&H was certainly nothing fancy, just a long counter and only a few tables. It was very old-school, about as old-school as it got in NYC anymore. But the borscht and the latkes and the pierogis were the best in the city. I took a seat at the counter. I told the waiter-slash-cook that I was waiting for a friend. He smiled and said suggestively, "A friend, a friend." Minh came in wearing a petunia-colored down jacket that went past her knees and matching white knitted scarf, gloves, and cap. She saw me and sat down on the stool next to mine. Taking off her cap and gloves, she stuck them in the pockets of her coat and then turned to me and smiled. It was the first time I had seen her face in its entirety. It was a good face, a beautiful face, and her smile was enchanting.

"This place is a museum. Museum quality," she said, taking it all in.

"Museum quality?"

"Because it is put together in such a way. All of these placards on yellow paper enclosed in clear plastic and stuck to the wall; the words on each one, words that mean how they sound. Reminds me of Barney's Beanery. I love it."

"Well, you don't find too many kosher diners from the 1940s anymore. Not even in New York City."

"No, not anymore."

"Even Barney Greengrass is gone," I said mournfully.

"Yes. Poor Barney Greengrass."

I suggested the borscht and latkes with sour cream and applesauce. "Sounds good to me," she said. Reaching for her glass of water, again, she inadvertently rubbed her elbow next to mine and once more a kind of static electricity. I could feel myself getting slightly aroused. It had been a long time since I had been near a woman, a lifetime. She was winsome and affecting, and she smelled terrific. Like flowers, like gardenias, like the essence of something good, like the core of grace.

"I haven't been to a movie in a while," she told me.

"I go all the time. I practically live at the Film Forum."

"Can I ask you a question?"

"A question? Yes, of course, anything."

"Anything?"

"Anything."

"Your name. Are you Vietnamese? Because you don't look it. And I should know."

"It's a long story. And the movie is starting soon. And it's probably better than my movie."

"I think I would like to see *your* movie."

"It's still being edited."

She laughed and it wasn't my feeble attempt at humor that she laughed at; it was something else because she looked at me, took a breath, and laughed again.

"What's so funny?" I asked her.

"Oh, nothing."

The Angelika East is an old-school movie palace designed in the Moorish Revival style about a hundred years earlier in what was formerly the Yiddish district. We sat in the balcony, front row, side by side. The film takes place in the 1970s in Southern California. So much of my past I don't remember. There are parts, sunspots, that I sometimes see in my mind's eye; of being about ten years old and living in the suburbs. The film strikes chords in me. The clothes, the cars, the awkward intersection between children and adults, the mendacious currents channeling in every part of the society. The cover-ups in politics, in marriages, rampant crime, serial killers, sitcoms on television attempting to mirror everyday life, the energy crisis, the aftereffects of the Vietnam War, the lingering trauma of the assassinations of Kennedy, King, and the other Kennedy, the specter of the A-Bomb, and rock music - Glam Rock, Punk Rock, Hair Rock, Goth Rock, all of it ripping through the culture.

I took her in from the corner of my eye and tried to sense how she was enjoying the film. But what I was really trying to discern was what she thought of me. Did she see through my facade? I was so tired of having one, and with this person, with this particular person, I wanted to reveal myself, at least all of what I knew for certain about myself. Only to her. Yet, there was so much that I could not recall. For instance, my precise age, my real name, where I grew up—aside from the fragments that remained in my memory. I remembered dying, and escaping, and traveling, and living in the desert, and then later coming in from the brush, hitchhiking across the country, stopping for months or maybe years at this place or that place, working this job in that factory before hitting the road again, getting jobs in restaurants as a busboy; any job that paid under the table because I had no ID. And then landing in New York City and lucking into a job at a bookstore. At Mercer Books.

Sometimes it comes back to me. I was in a great deal of pain. I did a lot of drugs, heroin. My heart, and the condition of equilibrium utterly shattered. This I know. The fragments of sense memory are still there. The sense memory of heartache. A flashing glimpse of me. My clothes piss-stained and full of shit and dirt. My face matted with detritus, a boho funk-clustered beard. My heart had stopped. My heart stopped, and I lay on the gurney in a dark hospital somewhere in Southern California. Two orderlies assigned to take care of my corpse had first needed to smoke a joint before doing so.

"We got to take care of this body first," I heard one say, my eyes firmly shut.

"It can wait."

"Yeah but . . ."

"Yeah but what? He's dead, isn't he?" And the one slapped my leg. "He's not going anywhere. The guy shot up enough heroin to kill an elephant."

"Yeah but . . ."

"Yeah but what?"

"Yeah but the shift supervisor is coming, and we've been fucking off a lot lately. I need this stupid job."

"He signed off. And a new one is not coming for another hour."

"Are you sure?"

"Totally."

"Let's go get high."

The two orderlies walked away to get high and I raised myself like Lazarus. I touched my arms with my hands, then I felt my face, my disgusting beard, and I knew what had happened. I instinctively knew that I had died; that I had OD'd, and had subsequently come to. But that was all I knew. I didn't know who I was or where I lived or what I did for a living. Still, judging by my utterly disheveled appearance, I imagined that I was a vagrant. I got off the gurney. My legs were wobbly. I held the gurney for support. Then I heard the two orderlies coming back, so I hid behind another gurney with another dead body on it.

"Where's the body? No kidding, it's gone."

"Don't be an idiot."

"Look for yourself."

The sound of a sheet being ruffled.

"What the fuck?"

"Check his chart. Maybe someone else got him."

The sound of papers being ruffled and the clipboard placed back on the gurney.

"Jesus fucking Christ. I'm not that high."

"Look, whatever happened, we just do what we were supposed to do. Put the body in the bag and the bag in the box. Body or no body. Let them take him, or what should be him, to Potter's Field, and let's be done with it. I got to get home and sleep this one off."

After they rolled the gurney away, I grabbed some scrubs hanging in the anteroom and made my way through the halls unnoticed. Finding an exit door, I left the building. It felt like the dead of night. I didn't know where I was. It looked like some deserted desert town. Possibly near Joshua Tree. I recognized those odd, ominous cacti resembling humans frozen in motion. I broke into the back of a thrift store and found some clothes and a pair of boots in my size—or close enough—and hit the road.

I walked until daylight and then hitched a ride from a lady driving an old Ford pickup truck. She had on jeans, a tee-shirt, and a black wig that sat on her head like a hat, yet resembled a cat. It made me laugh.

"You're happy," she said.

I nodded.

"Where are you going?"

I shrugged.

"Well, I am going to Salinas with this load of stuff. I'll drop you there."

I nodded.

"You're funny. And a bit disgusting. But I like you. I knew I liked you when I saw your disheveled character standing so erect and proud on the shoulder of this here I-5."

I smiled.

"You are a man not a mouse."

I gave her a curious look, a dog tilting its head.

"But the best laid plans of mice and men. Robert Burns, John Steinbeck. Have you read them?"

I shrugged.

She reached into the glove compartment and handed me a beat-up paperback of *East of Eden*. All the while keeping the wheels of the Ford straight and steady with her knees.

"Read that in the evenings after a long day's work picking kiwis."

"Picking kiwis?"

"Yes. That's where I am taking you. To my farm to pick

kiwis. I assume that's okay with you."

I shrugged, smiled, and then nodded.

I worked at the kiwi farm until the season ended. During that time the woman gave me books by Steinbeck, Erskine Caldwell, David Goodis, Walker Percy. I returned the books to her when I went to say goodbye. She thanked me for my work, and gave me an envelope full of money and a hard cover of Mary Shelley's *Frankenstein*. I opened the cover and on the first page was scrawled *To Louise – here's to new beginnings – Love Mary.*

CHAPTER 3

◆

After the movie we went to the wine bar across the street. She ordered a glass of Pinot Noir, and I asked for a glass of seltzer water. I rarely drank alcohol, and only when I was alone. I knew that wine or booze made one less inhibited, and I felt that I needed to be inhibited all the time. I had to be aware of my circumstances, of my location, of the people I was with, especially now that I had something to lose. On the other hand, having known emptiness and nothingness, and having had not even a penny, I knew how to get back there, I knew how to live that way. But I didn't want to. I was sick of it. I liked having money. I liked having an identity, even if it wasn't mine. It was part mine. It was mine in the sense that I had bought it. Like one buys a computer or a phone or a car.

She sat across from me, roseate and animated. My mind flickered. Each look, gesture, slowed so that I could take it in while everything else moved in real time. Her evocative and sagacious eyes, almost entities unto themselves, darted as I spoke; taking in my mouth, eyes, hands, hair; as if she were cataloging my movements as I spoke. And I took in the completeness of her face even as I gabbed nervously; her nose, philtrum, and lips, each pronounced and full, were of a unified whole; curious, intrepid, nonchalant, and interested—in me, it seemed. Her hands, small, delicate, with pearl-white polish on the nails, gestured and posed like one of those Alfred Stieglitz photos of Georgia O'Keeffe's hands. She had a little chuckle, caused her glasses to slip down her nose and with her index finger she'd put back up. All of it, all of her, was quite disarming. But because of that face, so open, I wanted to tell her everything about myself.

Diminutive, about five foot two, the wine was quickly getting her a little giddy. Her teeth were starting to take on a pinkish hue. To make conversation, out of nervousness, I told her about the few bad dates that new friends from the publishing house had set me up with, and how they had ended in embarrassment when, as a result of some awkward utterance on my part, the woman with whom I had been sharing company brought things to a quick close after the requisite dining experience was concluded. Which was fine with me. I was happy to get home to the company of Djuna Barnes, P. G. Wodehouse, Will Durant, Colette, or whoever it was that I was currently consumed by. I told Minh about one particularly embarrassing moment during a date when I told the woman I was with, with all seriousness, that I suspected that I was not born on this planet. That didn't go over well. She must have thought that I was a lunatic.

"Do you really think you were born on another planet?" Minh asked, laughing.

"I don't rule it out."

"Anything is possible. The thought has crossed my mind as well."

"You find these stories of my catastrophic dating experiences amusing, do you?" I asked Minh.

"Yes. Very."

"I'm so glad."

"I don't know about those women, but I like you."

"You do?"

"I do. I find you amiable, balanced, intelligent, and intriguing. I like that your face is spattered with freckles. Like an orange monochromatic Jackson Pollack. And, there's something about you. As if nothing could faze you."

"I don't know about that. But. One of the first things that I did when I came into some money as a result of my book deal was to see a shrink. You see, I had crippling bouts of guilt.

Such guilt."

"What did you feel guilty about?"

"That's what I wanted to find out. I went to this ancient shrink on the Upper East Side. A Doctor Finkelstein. I had read a few of his books. He survived the Holocaust as a boy. He lost his entire family but he survived, so I felt he would have some keen insight into my problem. With guilt."

"Did he? What did he say?"

"He said, 'Do you see zat vastebasket in za corner of my office?' He pointed to the corner of his office, where there was a black plastic wastebasket. He said, 'You take your guilt and throw it all into zat vastebasket, you hear?' I stood and did what he said, though I felt quite silly. I left his office feeling that I had just wasted two hundred dollars. Yet, I did feel lighter. And when I started feeling that strange anonymous guilty feeling again, I peel the guilt from off of me and rolled it into a ball and dropped it into my wastebasket."

"Does it work?"

"It actually does."

The waiter came over and asked if Minh wanted another glass of wine. She looked at the glass, which had a little wine left in it, and said somewhat loudly, "No thanks."

"Where do you live? I have a car."

"I live on the Upper West Side," she smiled. "It's near Columbia. Really great location."

"Do you want a ride home?"

"Sure, if it's not a bother. It's quite out of your way. You live in Brooklyn, after all."

On the ride to her place, we had a lively conversation about literature and our favorite writers. Hers: Marguerite Duras, Elena Ferrante, Philip Roth, Sally Rooney. Mine: Virginia Woolf, Edith Wharton, Lucia Berlin, and Philip Roth. She liked all the writers on my list as I liked all on hers. With Philip Roth being the touchstone.

Side by side we talked as if we had known each other for years instead of days. I took 14th Street to the West Side Highway. Driving along the Hudson River, a Miles Davis CD,

Friday Night in Person at the Blackhawk, San Francisco, Volume 1 in the player. Miles playing live with his great post-Coltrane/ Adderley combo with Wynton Kelly on piano. Miles's horn, often with a mute, like a voice singing the blues or a standard. It felt urbane and romantic, with Minh and her perfume and her singsong voice and her playful way of engaging me, it felt like a scene from a French movie from the late fifties.

Now the question in the forefront of my mind was: should I try to kiss her? When we get in front of her building, I'll put the car in park and ask. First ask permission. Something like this: "Would you mind if I kissed you?" No, that was an idiotic way of putting it. But how else could I phrase it? "I was thinking that it would be really nice to kiss you, do you mind?" God, even worse. Or, I could just lean over and try. First, however, I would have to unbuckle my seatbelt, which would take away the element of surprise. Surprise this young woman with an attempted kiss. She could, after all, bat me away if she wanted. Yet, why had she engaged me in conversation at Café Lux and so readily given me her phone number? And what was that electricity when we inadvertently touched elbows? Was it even inadvertent, or had she meant to make initial contact that way? Or maybe it was inadvertent and maybe it was just static electricity. And maybe she just wanted to go and see the movie with someone. She is a writer, she likes the idea of hanging out with another writer. On the other hand, she was in a writing program and she probably knows many writers her own age. And do I even want to kiss her, or was it just something I was expected to try and do? I did want to kiss her. I wanted to kiss her the second I saw her. I wasn't objectifying her, her body, age, and beauty. She was attractive, no doubt, yet what was most attractive about her were her eyes and her smile, and the way she found me entertaining in some way.

I pulled up to her corner, 69th and Amsterdam, just as Miles finished his solo on "If I Were a Bell." I thought, Now is the time, make the move and do it quickly. But no, I can't just make a move; you must ask permission. Before I could do anything, she said, "Well, thanks for the movie and the wine."

And she looked at me. I wasn't sure what the look meant. For the first time, her expression was somewhat ambiguous, at least to the extent that I could draw nothing from it. I could hazard no guesses. I simply said, "It was my pleasure." She opened the door of the car and got out. I watched her cross the street and go into her building. It started to rain lightly.

Driving down Amsterdam, I made a right on 59th Street, and then a left on the West Side Highway. I took off Miles and stuck in a CD of The Pretty Things' album *Parachute*. Electric guitars and vocal harmonies. Should I have at least tried to kiss her? No, obviously that expression—ambiguous, no, ambivalent—it said, "You better not try anything, buster." Albeit kindly.

But I am not looking for anyone and, in fact, prefer my way of being solo. Yet, I would like to find a woman to make love to, who asked no questions about who I was. I did not have any answers readily available on that subject anyway. I had done most of the talking with Minh. And I must say, she found my stories entertaining. What would she think of the real story? (What little of it I know.) I do know the story of my coming to NYC and what happened to me since I have been here. Which is probably not that different from a lot of people. You get to NYC and you strive.

I got home to my pad in Brooklyn. A two-bedroom apartment in Windsor Terrace. There was my dog, Humphrey, waiting for me. I took him out for a midnight walk. Humphrey, though only a year old, was quite skilled at holding his poo and pee for as long as eight hours. We went for a stroll in the light rain. I was wondering if it would snow. It was cold enough. I heard my phone go *bing*. I looked at the message. It was Minh: "I was sad that we didn't kiss."

CHAPTER 4

◆

I stood on a street in the West Village looking up at a crescent moon lingering directly beneath a sun obscured by gauzy clouds. I couldn't recall ever having seen such a thing before. The sun and the moon sharing the sky. Night and day merging. It was so beautiful I thought I might start weeping when I was knocked to the ground by a man with a beard, no mustache, and hair silver like moon glitter. He hurriedly helped me up and quite vexedly said, "What are you doing right now?" I shook my head. "Just looking at the sun and the moon." "Will you watch my bookstore? I need to kind of get the hell out of here. You see. There's a woman looking for me, going to come here, she is kind of vicious, she thinks that, well, me and her daughter, well. I need to beat a hasty retreat." I looked at the storefront he was pointing to, the window filled with art books on display. He took me inside and showed me how to use the register and the credit card machine. "Here are the keys, I'll be back later. And if I don't return, just lock the door and meet me at Chumley's and I'll pay you for the day." He took my hand, put the keys in it, and split. And that's where I lived and made a living for over a decade. In a basement bookstore on Mercer Street.

I had at my disposal every manner and topic of book. Books on philosophy, psychology, biology, art, art history, science, history, literary criticism, art criticism, poetry, photography, theology, and, of course, literature. The owner, the man who I met that first day, was named Charlie Button. He was tall, languorous, and had a red bulbous nose, probably as a result of his nightly whisky consumption with his friends, a group of rarely published writers. But they—as a group and individually—were undaunted and somewhat legendary. At least in the West Village. I got to know them all quite well.

Working for Charlie was like being born. He gave me keys and let me run the shop. Freed him to pursue the things that he pursued. Namely, young NYU students and more whisky. Language came back to me. The books coaxed me. Also the various street people who sold books. These were tragic figures, former professors or critics or writers or jazz or rock musicians who had developed drug addictions and became proficient at finding books, determining their value and selling the books to attain the next fix. They knew where to find the good stuff. Books, that is.

Because of being surrounded by books constantly, and because of my love of books, it seemed like we were merged. That is the idea of a book and my own story, personality, soul mechanism. The years passed. I did not keep track. When someone asked my age, I would conjecture: twenty-five, thirty-two, forty-four. How long was I in the wild? How old was I before I died?

Yet, I was most decidedly alive. Now. I simply wanted to partake in life as it came to me in the bookstore; the people and the books. Charlie had an extra room above the store. I stayed with him. He was not there often, nor was he at the bookstore. Over time, I became the sole employee, working there six days a week from 11:00 a.m. to 10:00 p.m. Charlie worked Sundays, or the store was closed on Sundays if he didn't make it. So, I would open it. It was fine. I had no place to go.

Sometimes I would go out after the store was closed to hear jazz or poetry or folk music. The Village still retained those elements. The Village still retained its character. So many bemoan how the city has lost its character and identity, still I found it readily. There I was, like a toddler finding my balance; immediately given the keys to my livelihood. And a key to an apartment, and a key to understanding who I am, and by that, some understanding in regard to who I was. But it was still opaque, and so, like that toddler, as I discovered the world around me, the elements of the city formed my distinct whole.

CHAPTER 5

◆

Once you've been dead, and then come back, you can interpret it as a missed opportunity. A missed opportunity for whom? For fate to be sure. But also a missed opportunity to find out what lies beyond, if anything. I got a glimpse to be sure, and yet I feel that glimpse can only be interpreted as a fragment from the dream state. I saw no tunnel of light nor great white-bearded grandfather awaiting me with open arms. No Jesus. All I saw was a stellar landscape of white, and black, and my mother, and then the many lives that I might have lived. All of it slipped past in seconds, in years. Now as I write from the future, looking to the past, from the vantage of the present—where everything has changed in such utterly remarkable ways. Not just my life. Everything. The conditions of society, of the world, of climate, of culture, of transcendental evolution; the civilization as a whole has undergone a great transformation. There has been an extraordinary turn of events. And I think people from the past, who were living in the present day of 2025, I think that those people, including myself, would have a great deal of difficulty grappling with the truth of this present day: December 15th, 2035.

I texted Minh that I wished to correct that. That missed opportunity. I felt stupid. After all, isn't that something I should have sensed and pursued? As a man? Though, it is an odd configuration in the front seat of a car, to maneuver around, lean and reach across, grab hold of a shoulder to draw her nearer? That seemed aggressive, and foreign to my sensibilities. But still, I didn't even try. I texted back awkwardly. "Yes, I would very much like to kiss you. When can I see you again?"

"I am going to Boulder, Colorado, to visit relatives." To Colorado and wouldn't be back for two weeks. So my missed opportunity would have to wait for at least two weeks. We talked on the phone while she was away. Her voice sounded younger on the phone than in person. I could see her smile in my mind. She explained that her relatives in Boulder were the only family that she had in the States; the rest of her family was back in Hanoi.

"What do you do? In Boulder?"

"I am primarily just reading and writing, and working on a short story, or really a fragment from my novel."

"What's it about?"

"It's a story about a trip I took with a friend. We went to Miami to spend a weekend and take in the glitz of that semi-decadent place. I was curious about 'the epitome of the American Dream.'"

"Is that what Miami is?"

"It's been said," she said sardonically. "Being from Vietnam I am curious about the subject. In the story the friend says she is leaving, and the young woman, the protagonist of the story, decides to stay and see the place by herself, making observations —alone. She meets an older woman in an upscale bar. The woman is a bit of a lush but glamorous in dress and gesture, and she takes quite a liking to the young woman of the story. She tells her that she has magic in her eyes. And in the story, the younger woman meets the eccentric acquaintances of the elder, characters who by the end of the night the older woman, intoxicated by champagne cocktails, has effectively antagonized, so that it is just the protagonist and herself left alone."

"What happens then?"

"I'm still working on it."

"Is it based on your own experiences?"

"Yes."

"Sounds fascinating," I told her. My voice earnest, because it was.

Gone for two weeks, now a disembodied voice. I did have

a face to place it, mostly half a face: from Café Lux, B&H, Angelika East, and my car, where only her profile had been visible to me. Only in the wine bar did I see her full face. Yet it resonated, and I could see it clearly in my mind's eye. During those two weeks, I ruminated on it, on her. Why was I doing that? What was happening to me? Had I gotten looser with my inclination to be separate from the crowd, my vow to be insular, to be cloaked in anonymity except when it came to creating a persona for my fiction and for my fictive human being? Being a human, if that's what I truly was?

This woman. Smart, fresh with language and ideas, precocious to the point of not caring much about things like the difference in our ages. She is a writer, and I am a writer. Though for me, I feel that I am and perhaps I am not. As is the case with all who have invented themselves, the thought that one could be found out. Be called a charlatan. John Cheever invented his persona, his own accent. Part Bloomsbury, part New England aristocrat, part white trash. I had invented mine by watching Charlie's VHS-tape collection of Hollywood movies from the 1930s. William Powell in the *Thin Man* series, Humphrey Bogart, Clark Gable, Cary Grant, an amalgamation of the syntax of dashing leading men.

Minh would be back from Colorado on the day after Christmas. Because she was from Vietnam, I assumed Christmas meant nothing to her. But I was wrong; she, just like most people in this country, had a sentimental attachment to the holiday. After all, she had been in America since she was fourteen, having gotten a scholarship to attend a fancy boarding school in Pennsylvania. Christmas meant nothing to me, aside from enjoying Christmas movies such as *It's a Wonderful Life, Miracle on 34th Street,* and *Remember the Night,* which usually played at Film Forum that time of year. I sometimes went in the evenings after work. Or on a Sunday. On a Sunday I might see two, possibly three, and sometimes even four films if the timing worked out. Now, I felt that I was starring in a film of my own. A great New York City Christmas love story.

I told her to meet me at the Waverly Inn for dinner. I only

felt comfortable in the establishments that had withstood the tests of time. Those were primarily the places that I frequented. I thought that as a writer she would appreciate the mural that adorned the main dining room, since it was populated by famous and infamous writers. Perhaps one day we would join that pantheon. And why not. Anything was possible. The fact that we had even met I would have considered wildly unlikely. Or that I would have met someone like her. I didn't know that someone like her existed. Still, we had met, and it was bewildering me.

CHAPTER 6

◆

I sat at a table by the fireplace in the front room of the Waverly Inn waiting for her to arrive. I ordered a seltzer, which I sipped while I made notes in my red notebook. Not notes for the novel. It was a mere list describing the contents of the room. The fireplace, the men and women at the bar chatting amiably. The maître d' elegantly dressed in his black suit and bow tie taking inventory of the small crowd. I described my anxious anticipation as a warm piece of clothing. A red wool sweater. Minh arrived; she looked around nervously until she spotted me, and then that smile, so natural and authentically gleeful.

We looked at the menus. I never know the etiquette in regard to ordering on a date. Cocktails, appetizers, and other nonsense. Minh put down the menu and said, as if she were sharing a secret, "When I told my hairdresser, Clint, that I was going to the Waverly Inn, he said that I must try the mac and cheese." Her hair. That was what was different about her: feathered at the tips and cut to frame her face like a laurel. I looked at her, so beautiful and young, with intelligent eyes. I had to wonder if I was in the right place; had there been some kind of cosmic mistake?

"What? Oh yes. I love mac and cheese," I said, feeling glad that the awkwardness of ordering had been settled by there being something on the menu in which we both were interested. She added matter-of-factly, "I'll have oysters and a glass of champagne, as well." I nodded.

The waiter, traditionally attired in white shirt, bow tie,

and black vest and attitude, approached us. He took the order and repeated it back to me, slowly and deliberately enunciating, "Truffled mac and cheese," as if he were repeating a marriage vow.

Minh reminded me of Holly Golightly. Or Audrey Hepburn as Holly. A Vietnamese Holly/Audrey. Something unmistakably playful about her general demeanor. Which struck a bell. As if we were both playing dress-up.

I must have come to the Waverly a half dozen times. By myself, and had dinner by myself. I often wondered what it would be like to have company. The company of a beautiful woman. Or any woman. She needn't be beautiful. Merely intelligent. Someone who liked books and art and music and cinema and loved New York City. And here she was. I wondered, what's the catch? There seemingly was no catch. And even if there was, what did I care? I lived each day as if I had nothing to lose. I truly had nothing to lose. Everything was gravy. I had died and been given another life. Yet—I had everything to lose.

I tried an oyster upon her insistence. At first I couldn't see the attraction. Strange thing, moist, glistening, looking like a lymph node, though attractively displayed on a half shell designed to perfectly slide the thing into one's mouth and, with a minimal amount of mastication, down one's throat. Not a great deal of flavor yet there was something quite pleasant about the taste. Even sensuous. What was really sensuous was the way Minh held the shell, her hand poised like an aristocrat, showed me a smile, and slid the little shimmering glob beyond her crimson lips.

"Which one is your favorite?" she asked me quizzically.

"How do you mean?"

"The writers, on the mural. Of them, do you have a favorite?"

Because my back was facing the mural I had to turn to take a look. "Oh. That's a difficult choice. I just read *Giovanni's Room.* I was shattered by it."

"Shattered?"

"Yes. Very much so. Also exhilarated. So tragic. I am often stopped cold by how cruel life can be. But from the vantage of having been given so much. Baldwin is a fascinating man."

"Do you identify with him?"

Ignoring the underlying implication in her question, I responded, "Only in the idea that one has to go someplace else from where you originated to find and be the person you were meant to be. In his case Baldwin went to Paris."

"He eventually returned."

"Yes, but only after he was able *to be*."

"A writer."

"A person." After a brief break in the conversation, I ventured, "How about you?"

"I like Baldwin, too. *Another Country* was formative. Being from Vietnam and having lived in the U.S. for all of my adult life, actually since I was a teen, I feel the alienation he writes about. In a different way, of course. I identify with Giovanni. And the way Baldwin depicts the whites in the book, how they always downplay racism. I have experienced that. Given a choice though, I'd take Edna St. Vincent."

"Does your candle burn at both ends?"

"Oh, gosh no. I do like her line, let's see, how does it go? 'I am glad that I paid so little attention to good advice; had I abided by it I might have been saved from my most valuable mistakes.'"

"Yes. That's good," I said. "So, you like poetry?"

"No. I hate it," she said seriously. Then smiled and said, "But I haven't heard enough good poetry, and have heard a lot of truly wretched poetry."

The mac and cheese arrived. We didn't waste time commenting on how beautiful it looked in the clay pot, the chiaroscuro of the almost burnt cheese in a wavy sea of golden noodles. Simultaneously we dug in. "Why is it so good?" I asked Minh. "Why, it's the truffles. You know, there is a kind of pig, they call it a truffler, you need one of these pigs to find the truffles, which lie hidden beneath the ground."

"OK. You're making this up."

"No, I'm not. Really."

I smiled and continued eating.

She asked me, "If you could live anywhere in time, where would you live?"

"I would live in the late fifties, early sixties New York City, when American culture was at its apex. When it had blossomed to fruition. The New York School of poetry: Frank O'Hara, John Ashbery, Kenneth Koch, Joe Brainard. The great novelists: Mary McCarthy, Saul Bellow, Philip Roth, Norman Mailer. Broadway was producing groundbreaking musicals like Leonard Bernstein's *West Side Story*, and the modern jazz of Miles Davis, John Coltrane, Thelonious Monk, and the plays of Eugene O'Neill, Arthur Miller, don't forget the abstract expressionists—Pollock, Joan Michell, de Kooning, and *everyone* gathering at Cedar Tavern."

"There he is," Minh said, looking at my glass.

"There who is?" I asked.

"Norman Mailer."

"But, but, he's dead."

Touching the coaster beneath my glass of seltzer. "Yes, I know. He's on the paper coaster under your glass."

"Oh yes. I forgot about that. From when he ran for mayor. He's another American self-made myth. His life was probably even more interesting than anything he wrote."

"Didn't he stab his wife?"

"Yes. He did that. I didn't say he was necessarily a good fellow."

"Well, we all lead flawed lives. To a certain extent."

"Yeah. But stabbing your wife is beyond the pale. What about you? What's your favorite time and place?"

"Oh. I would say, Paris, turn of the century, before the great war. I would love to be Sylvia Beach and own my own bookstore."

"Wouldn't you rather be the writer of books in the store?"

"Yes, that too," she said laughing.

"I know what you mean. It just might be every writer's secret fantasy to own their own bookstore. I worked in a bookstore for years."

"You did? Which one?"

"Mercer Books. My first day in New York I was given the keys."

"Oh my gosh."

"I worked there, really was the only employee, until last year when I got the book deal. It was practically like living in a library. Every kind of book and recording at my fingertips."

"Sounds like heaven."

"In so many ways it was. It felt like I had died and gone to heaven. Now, it's a different chapter. I'm out in the world. Before I wasn't. Not so much. In fact. I'm going to Paris."

Her eyes lit up, "You are. When?"

"End of January, beginning of February."

She spoke rapidly, "I love Paris. I went to French school as a kid. I speak it fluently."

"I don't speak a word. Yet I am a confirmed Francophile. I love French music, films, novels, and poetry." And before I knew what I was saying I said, "You should come. I've rented a flat in the Latin Quarter."

"Really?"

"Yeah, sure, why not."

"Okay then."

And we each took a bite from our clay dishes, finishing the truffled mac and cheese.

CHAPTER 7

◆

We ordered the bananas Foster for dessert, harkening back to our first encounter and the banana mousse. The rum was strong. It seemed to preponderate the giddiness I was feeling. Giddy at having stumbled upon someone who shared so many interests and sensibilities yet also feeling a very strong attraction and sensing that in the other. Which got me thinking about our first kiss. Now that the ground was laid, it was implicit that a kiss between us was what was going to happen. It seemed like she was thinking about the same thing. A sort of coy smile played on her lips, as she sat back after we finished the dessert. Smiling back at her, I could barely conceal my expectancy. I turned around and raised my arm to signal the waiter and said, "Check!" a little too loudly, which made Minh laugh.

After a busboy took the empty plate, the waiter came and ceremoniously placed the check in front of me. I had brought a lot of cash in order to make an impression. Five crisp one-hundred-dollar bills. Assuming I would spend half of that on dinner, and then have more for a drink and perhaps a jazz club afterward. I had a debit card yet I kept most of my cash in savings. It all felt like stolen money, even though I had earned every cent. I turned over the bill. My face turned red. The bill was for seven hundred dollars. Minh saw the number and put her hand to her mouth. "There must be a mistake," she said.

The waiter came over. I repeated Minh's words to him. "There is no mistake, sir."

"But, it says here two hundred and fifty dollars apiece for

the mac and cheese."

"Truffled mac and cheese, sir."

"Yes, truffled. But haven't you added an extra zero?"

"That is the price, sir."

"Yes but," Minh said, "we only ordered one."

"You seem to have eaten two. Two empty pots of mac and cheese were removed from your table."

"But we only ordered one," Minh insisted.

"Let me call the manager over," the waiter said petulantly.

"Listen," I said. "Come here," and I motioned for the waiter to lean down so that I might whisper something in his ear. After I finished he nodded and walked away. "Let's go." Minh stood. I helped her with her coat. I put five one hundred dollar bills on the table and we left.

We strolled at a leisurely pace down Bank Street toward where I had parked my car on Bleecker. Bank Street hadn't changed much in the last two hundred years. A skinny one-way street, running east to west, row houses made of brick and limestone huddled together, and a variety of trees lining the sidewalk. I decided to recite all of the trees to Minh. "Look, there's a Callery pear, and a thornless honey locust, a willow oak, a Japanese zelkova, of course a ginkgo, and there's a sawtooth oak," pointing across the street, "there's a hedge maple, and a London planetree, that's a sweet gum, and a Japanese flowering tree, a Japanese pagoda tree, and lastly an American elm. That's a wide variety of trees in just a two-block radius. I read a book about the trees of the West Village. Here's my car."

She looked a little irritated. We both knew what was on the agenda. The kiss. The kiss that wasn't and was to be. And I was obviously delaying. I knew I couldn't stall any longer. I thought of only one way to do this. She looked up at me. I'm not tall, medium. Five foot ten. She, I reckoned, was about five two. I leaned down, she raised her head, and I kissed her. It was anticlimactic. To say the least. Like how it might be to kiss your cousin or sister or aunt. Tight-mouthed. I didn't try to loosen things and I pulled away. I wasn't very experienced in these matters, yet was experienced enough to know that there was no inherent kinetic energy there. I reached inside my pocket for the keys to the car.

I started the engine. I had already loaded a Chet Baker CD in the deck. Chet singing "Bewitched, Bothered, and Bewildered." I thought it over and it occurred to me that perhaps we were both a little nervous. She might have been thinking the same thing because she said, "Can we try it again?" I put my arm around her and pulled her nearer and put my lips on hers. She was more receptive this time. Her lips were full and moist and she was passionate. She put her hand on my forearm to pull me even closer. We kissed until the CD played all the way through and Chet started singing "Bewitched" again.

CHAPTER 8

◆

In Paris, we got set up in a garret in the Latin Quarter which I found in the back pages of the *New York Review of Books*. One of the reasons that I was going to Paris was to see my friend Jean-Claude Duffet, a stride pianist of some acclaim. As it turned out he was away on a tour of the Antibes. I had met Jean-Claude years before in a small speakeasy on the Lower East Side where I was asked to read some poems. Jean-Claude played the late night set and had come early to get a few drinks under his belt. He listened to my poems which were all quite purple. Not that I had been having sexual relations with anyone. Yet, I liked to think about it and write about it. Wish fulfillment. Someone I could lift up, someone where we could fulfill a need in each other. *And as the dust of the ancients filled our lungs, we spoke, and this was a sign of everlastingness.* Jean-Claude liked all of that and asked me to write lyrics to a few of his melodies. Every time he came to town we hung out.

Minh and I stayed in the Latin Quarter and got to know each other. The way you get to know someone when you sleep next to them for consecutive nights, something I had never done, at least not in my current state of recollection. You and your partner have dreams and make sounds in sleep, and then you listen and they reach for you and you are there and you touch them and then hold them and you get aroused, she reaches for my cock and holds it like it is hers. And it gets very hard and she is very wet, so you make love—again.

We also got to know each other in a surface way. Though

we spent time together talking, having lengthy discussions about the world and our place in it. I was gradually opening up about my story, though I had the feeling that she knew it by the way she nodded her head in affirmation each time I revealed something about myself. She would even say, "I know." I didn't bother asking her how she knew, but she knew. And as bits of her journey came forward, I could see that we had certain things in common. Namely, we were both outsiders.

The difference was, among many, she spoke three languages and was learning Italian when we met. She left Hanoi when she was fourteen after receiving a scholarship to an elite boarding school in Pennsylvania. She had essentially been on her own since then, though she stayed in close contact with her parents and older brother, usually spending a month or two in Hanoi during summers. She received a scholarship to an Ivy League school, and later another for postgraduate studies at Columbia. By sheer will, by the force of her intellect and ambition, she was able to impress those who parceled out those academic prizes. She won awards for plays, poems, and short stories. She had accomplished much and she had yet to turn twenty-seven when we met.

During the day we would set out for a museum, the Pompidou or Musée d'Orsay. We would never get there because just walking along the Seine or through the quiet winter streets was art enough. In the evenings we would unabashedly do the corny things literary tourists had been doing for decades; we would go to Café de Flore and Les Deux Magots, sit side by side in the outdoor seating area, reading or jotting in notebooks, smoking cigarettes, occasionally reading a passage from whatever book we had in hand. She was reading Rachel Cusk and I Duras. We were comfortable just being side by side and only making conversation when inspired to do so. Then we would go back to the flat, make love, and then out to dinner and then back to the flat again and make love until we fell asleep, wake up in the middle of the night and make love again.

Jean-Claude came back from tour and we went on double dates with Jean-Claude and his girlfriend, Sara, who happened to be the same age as Minh. Jean-Claude is not as old as me, though in the same ballpark. Born in Paris, Jean-Claude had the skinny on all the legit haute cuisine establishments. Jean-Claude told hilarious jokes making fun of French Canadians. Or dirty jokes not wholly acclimated to the political climate that made Sara and Minh laugh hysterically. I laughed at their enjoyment of Jean-Claude's performances, more so than his silliness. I had never laughed so much in my life.

One night after dinner with Jean-Claude and Sara, he invited us to hear him perform at a speakeasy called Lulu White's in the Place de Clichy. We all loaded into Jean-Claude's minivan. When we got to the club I helped him unload a beat-up spinet piano from the back of his minivan and into the club. We sat at the bar with Sara, basking in the ambience and the music as if we had stepped back in time. It felt like a dream, a dream in black-and-white; Minh beaming at the music, me beaming at Minh.

At Charles de Gaulle on our way back to New York we boarded the plane and got seated; me at the window and Minh in the middle. Minh had brought a small container of macarons for us to share. An older white woman sat down on the aisle seat. She looked at Minh scornfully and then made a comment under her breath: "I hope that's not sushi." It didn't fully register with me. The cruelty and intent of the comment, or it was just so flagrantly racist that I could not fully comprehend. I turned to Minh and asked, "Did she really just say that?" Minh did a deadpan expression, and then smiled and said, "She is obviously a very unhappy woman."

We sat on the tarmac for two hours, which felt like fate had conspired to bring the whole dreaminess of the trip to a crashing and tedious halt. In preparation for the reality of going back to New York City. Minh held my hand and we chatted about all of the wonderful things we had seen and done and this ameliorated a minor case of claustrophobia I was battling. Yet the comment of the woman was gnawing at me. I said, "I'm going to say something to that woman." She patted my hand like I was ten years old and said, "It's alright, I've heard worse. Really."

CHAPTER 9

◆

The first thing Minh did when we got back from Paris was break it off. She sent me a text: *Can we talk? On the phone?* That could only mean one of two things in my mind: either she was pregnant, which I felt was unlikely but possible, or she was ending it. She began the conversation with the words "I admire you so much." I knew it was over.

I knew it was over for so many reasons. Apart from the fact that I was older than her, I was intangibly opaque. I lacked any reasonable definition. The facts of my life did not add up. Not to her, and not to me. "Well," I said, almost snidely, "We will always have Paris." I ended the call.

Was I mad? No. Not really. Maybe a little. We had just had the most wonderful time imaginable, the most romantic and fun Paris trip, for two lovers, for two smart, bookish, romantically inclined lovers. We had made love for hours and had climax after climax. Was returning to a dingy dirty city by Parisian standards anticlimactic by comparison? In Paris I treated her royally; meals at five-star Michelin restaurants, museums, concerts. Mostly she liked to do what I always wanted to do, and that was to go to Café de Flore and sit side by side, sipping a drink and reading, not even talking to each other, just reading. The whole trip was perfect. And I knew she felt the same. So the only thing that I could figure was she wanted to end things on a high note, on the highest note. And seeing how things could only go downhill from Paris, it was smart. To end it. Still, it pissed me off.

I was back to my former self. Back to being alone. I knew when I told her: "I like being with you better than I like being alone." I knew that was trouble because it was true, even though I didn't believe myself at the time. Suddenly, and it was sudden, my world of blissful solitude, ruined. The whole ideology behind it was wrecked. God damn, Minh. Why did you have to talk to me in Café Lux? Why did you have to go to Paris with me? Why did I have to fall in love with you? Is that what happened? I fell in love? How could that be? What the hell was that?

In a panicked state I texted her: *please don't ghost me.* She wrote back that she never would. Well okay. That was my greatest fear when she broke things off, even though I didn't realize it at the time: that she would ghost me. I wrote her an email. I told her that I loved her. I confessed that I didn't know what the word meant. What does it mean? I asked rhetorically. Who knows? Still, I love you. I told her that I respected her, I respected her decision, but I hated it. I hated not seeing her. Every day. I wrote to Jean-Claude who said that I needed to send her flowers. I told him that I didn't know her address. I knew where she lived, just not her apartment number. Besides, she had made up her mind, and I needed to respect that. And there was the age difference. Jean-Claude said that is why I needed to try harder. He said that Sara had done the same thing to him, and he told her that you had to get burned if you wanted to live. I asked him if his tactic had worked, and he said it had. Probably sounded better in French.

Texting Minh, I asked her for her apartment number, which she sent. I didn't send her flowers. I sent her a record player, a Django Reinhardt and a Billie Holiday record. And letters. Many letters filled with poems and thoughts and recollections of our time together. I waxed philosophical about the idea of love. The mysteries of it. I never pleaded with her to take me back or reunite with me. I told her that I just needed to write to her until I got it out of my system. Until I got her out of my system.

One night, about a month after she had broken things off, I had been doing what had become routine every evening:

smoking cigarettes on the Williamsburg Bridge. They tasted so good. Cigarettes. The smoke meshed with heartache and melancholy formed an inner balm. After smoking half a pack I'd get in the Benz and drive all over East Williamsburg, Greenpoint, Bushwick, ultimately heading back to Windsor Terrace. Somewhere in Bed-Stuy my phone rang. It was Minh.

"Hello?"

"Hi. It's Minh."

"Yes."

"What are you doing?"

"Killing time, looking at the moon, contemplating bridges, ruffling my hair."

She said, "You have your New York voice on."

"What do you mean?"

"You sound, I don't know, cold."

"I have been smoking cigarettes."

"I got your letters."

"Oh. That's good. What do you think?" I said, trying to sound nonchalant.

"About what?"

"I don't know, the moon, bridges, Lenny Bruce, Belle and Sebastian, Stanislavsky."

"I like them. In fact, I love them."

"Do you love . . . No. Never mind."

"Do I love what?"

"Love me?"

"I love everything about you."

"Then why in God's name?"

"Did you get my letter?"

"No."

"You'll probably get it today. Or tomorrow. It's not as good as your letters. It's not poetry. But it explains things. Maybe a little better."

CHAPTER 10

◆

I was asked to organize a poetry reading. Harry Gribbs, who used to run the poetry reading at Mercer Books before I took it over, asked me to read. It was to be at a photography gallery on the Lower East Side. Harry had been published in *The New Yorker, Harper's, Paris Review*, et cetera. His books had been published by Little Brown, all five of them. Five books of poetry spread out over five decades. Needless to say, Harry didn't have much money. He didn't teach, he didn't have any job. What he had was a rent-controlled apartment that he had inherited from his beatnik parents, so the meager earnings of his books of poetry, which were all still in print, sustained him. He didn't need much. Yet he was a lovely poet. He wrote about solitude and urban architecture and the West Village and the people he knew and the lovers that he had known and his parents and his many cats. Somehow, he made it all very interesting.

Harry asked me to read and invite a photographer, if I'd like, to show images projected on the screen behind me. I didn't know any photographers so, with my phone, I shot steam coming out of the manholes in the streets of NYC. Mostly Upper East Side, where I often went to take in museums and walk around the reservoir. I liked it there. The buildings and wealthy old people with their little inbred dogs, fur coats, and facelifts. I dug that it was so unhip.

And so, behind me, I projected the video of ascending steam as I read this poem:

new york city
the naked city
naked and full of oratory
divine, splendid, tenacious
fatuous,
pulsing ppppulsating
beating in duple, triple
quadruple meter
quarter time half time
three quarters time
triple quintuple time
no time at all
there is no time in new york city
i love you
i love i love you
a city
your fluctuating thermal energy
undulating thermal energy
wild at times
unpredictable mercurial
gentle sweet lacerating
knock the hat off your head
knock the fucking hat off your head
what is joseph beuys without a hat?

ugly beauty all around
thelonious monk song
ugly beauty
written about you
at least in my mind
and then you drug us
intoxicate us with your mélange
quick blips of music
poetry heart arts
i love you new york city
and love is a real thing
like a stone or gall stones

sutures you need taken out
naked city weegee named you
because of your violence and sex
sexiness
i love you so much
at times it hurts
it hurts
and when you hurt i hurt
i have seen you hurt
attacked ravaged set on fire blown up
and when you hurt i hurt
because i love you
and i hate you too
the way you destroy the past
destroy the present
tear down and
wreck memory
but mostly
i love you
i love you am in love with you
and that is why
that is why i came to a decision
i decided
that
that
that
new york city
the naked city
would be my love
my one and only love

she was the one i loved—loved in that way
she understood anxiety
smoking a cigarette in the middle of the night
and i decided it would be just her and me me and her
she says the most beautiful exotic erotic things words songs
images in my eyes and ears

full of wind and past loves who flee into the reedy past
not keeping in the present long enough to mope
devoted i was devoted i am
to dining alone—except for her
the splendid restaurants bars and nightclubs
with my little red notebook
scrawling notes and ideas all in devotion to her
i discovered opera or she discovered me
pinnacle of music and dramaturgy
of song of pain of joy
café luxembourg and then the met
that was my routine
tosca porgy and bess
don carlos
at the café luxembourg
scrawling in my red notebook

and then one night
they sat me next to another lone diner
who i only saw through my periphery
but i felt her energy
maybe it was my own
i kept writing
in the red book I scrawled
notes for a screenplay
title took from a
silvina ocampo story
one of her characters asks another
what would you rather
love or be loved?
to love—
to give it without any expectation
of receiving it back
or be the one who is loved
with no guarantee
that you could return it

the periphery
asked if i was a writer
and i told her that i was
and

she was a writer as well
and liked to dine alone as well
and not only that
she went to the opera alone too
so we had that in common
she gave me her number
and made a plan to see each other
thirty years younger though
but what had me really concerned
somebody might have their heart hurt
and it would probably be me
and that's okay
but i was betraying my love
and the pact we had

the naked city said
do whatever the fuck you want
i said to myself
what do you want?
you were perfectly perfectly happy
just you and the naked city
but you can't fuck a city
even a naked city
even though the city can fuck you

speak to you
i talk to you
i speak to you in my mind
you are not there
you are in paris
i am in paris
i hold you

you hold me
we sleep that way
and then come apart and
then back together again
in a cloud
or an oscular bubble
always
this oscular bubble
like a keepsake
how could that have happened
never before have i spent so many
consecutive days
so perfect
each moment
and now
and now i am dizzy

and we returned
and i knew she knew we knew
because the city was at its most dingy
snow, black snow vomited all over the place
couldn't go back

she said
thank you
for taking me to paris
i thought
but did not say
i didn't take you—
you took yourself
you bought your own ticket
because you are a writer too
and a writer needs material
especially if she doesn't have much
i thought but did not say
said—you're welcome

and then
only a day after
we returned from paris
came the text
can we talk?

as prophesied
in an earlier poem
somebody is going to get
their heart broken
and i would rather it be me

and it was

i wondered
would new york city
take me back
after i had betrayed her
with another lover
and another city

but of course she did
unquestioningly
and i returned
to café luxembourg
me and my red notebook
though now it is a black moleskine
and then to the metropolitan opera house
alone

CHAPTER 11

◆

To see and to recognize truth and then to do what one must do when one is in the proper state of mind, the mind of a poet. Or telling oneself such. But, what truth? Whose truth? I loved this woman, her name is Minh. That was true, that was truth. And I wondered, had I been in love before this? Before I died. I couldn't be certain. It felt eerily familiar and yet not. Part of it made me have a headache and nausea. Part of it was like what it must feel like to take heroin. I have taken heroin and lots of it, so much that it killed me. But I don't remember what that felt like, what it felt like to die or to take heroin or to be in love.

The letter arrived the day after the poetry reading. In it Minh told me her reasoning which was logical and conventional. She acknowledged that someday she might want to get married and have a family and she figured that was something I had no interest in. Being so self-sufficient, so in need of privacy and solitude. Which she completely understood. She reiterated that she loved everything about me: the outward way I projected myself, my sartorial style, my invented brogue, my self-education and my appreciation of the arts and literature, my taste in music from opera to jazz, and most of all, how we fit so perfectly and seamlessly. She reasoned that she had to look to the future and didn't want to hurt me when the time came for her to settle down. If she met a man who could take care of her and provide for her and was willing and able to be a father to her children. So that is why she ended it. On a high note, on the highest note possible.

It made sense. Made complete sense. But she had never mentioned the age difference. And she assumed that what she desired was not something that I would be amenable to. And if posed the hypothetical scenario I probably would have said, right, no, not me. With Minh it was different. Would I want that? Would I be willing to share my life, my home, my resources? Of course I would. I loved her. Or thought that maybe I did. I hadn't quite spent enough time contemplating what that meant. Even though I had spent a lot of time contemplating what that meant. What is it, what is love? Is it a feeling? Is it logical? Is it the sum of all of its parts? When put together is this divine connection between two individuals what is called love, anything more than whimsy? No. It is more than whimsy. And yes, divine: holy, because it came down from a higher place, it has no body, has no physical presence aside from the physicality of making love—and everyone knows you can do that without it. Without love. Yes, I loved Minh. I loved her because I was willing to let her go. Yet not without telling her first that I loved her and would love to share a life with her. I put that in a letter and sent it to her

Right after this, I stopped sending her emails and texts, and letters. She wanted something more, perhaps more than I could give. I said that I was willing to be that person, but deep inside myself I wasn't sure if that was even possible. So I stopped and tried as best as I could to go back to my previous mode of existence.

One evening my phone buzzed. It was her.

"What are you doing?" she asked.

"I am reading Edith Wharton, *Glimpses of the Moon*, listening to Gil Evans's *Out of the Cool*. And thinking about you as usual."

"You are?"

"I am. I always am."

"Do you want to see me?"

"I want that. With every fiber of my being. Where are you?"

"I am in the Flatiron. I just finished dinner at Eataly."

"Do you want me to come and pick you up?"

"Yes. Very much."

In the car with Humphrey the dog, a little terrier poodle mutt who I had since acquired upon moving to Windsor Terrace, I drove excitedly to meet Minh. Minh told me that she knew I was a nice guy because my dog was so lovely and loving. I thought I'd bring him along to make her feel extra glad she asked me to pick her up. I parked on 24th Street and then walked to the entrance of the restaurant. Waiting for her to appear I got to thinking, it had been a month since I had last seen her. I had looked at the pictures on my phone from Paris, yet because of her face, the way it had so many different expressions, depending on the angle, on the light, on all criteria, I felt I couldn't trust it, the images could never capture someone so fluid. I had to rely on my mind's eye, but even that was only a mere filament. Barely tangible. Who was this person? Was she even real? Had I created her? Of course she was real, but was the person who I thought I was in love with real? It had been a month. A fucking month. The mind and memory and recollection can play games with someone. Nobody knew this better than me.

The full moon shone above the buildings of the Flatiron. Was it waxing or waning? Was I waxing or waning? Felt like I was waxing. Felt like I had been waxing for some time. We stood on the sidewalk, Humphrey and I. Suddenly, she came through the doors of the restaurant, radiant as always. As graceful, as intelligent, and beautiful as always, and coyly attempting to contain her pleasure at seeing me.

We held hands on the car ride back to Brooklyn. Barely spoke. Trading glances at the stoplights.

Glances, smiles, and a few tears. We got home and went to bed immediately. I kissed her everywhere. Everywhere I had kissed her before and places I hadn't kissed her yet. Kneecaps, elbows, armpits, wrists, ankles, and she seemed to get a tremendous amount of pleasure from each kiss, from each caress. When we had exhausted our passion we fell into a deep sleep.

"This doesn't mean we are back together," she said.

"Were we ever together?"

"Well, you know. I don't think we should continue seeing each other."

"I think we should."

"No. It's no good."

"Yes, your letter made sense. But I have a response."

"It's not just what I stated in the letter. More than that is that I don't know you. I know you based on what we have experienced together. And I love that. But I don't know you. Where you come from. Who your people are. Seems like there is some dark secret, and it is not my business to ask you to reveal anything that you don't want to reveal. So, I think it's best ..."

"I *want* to reveal. I want to reveal everything about myself. Everything that I know. I want to tell you. I have never told anyone. And I want to tell you. I have wanted to tell you since the first time I saw you," I said, attempting to keep the urgency and potential heartbreak out of my already cracking voice.

"You don't have to."

"I know. I am ready to. I want to. And if after I tell you you still want to end things I will respect that. I won't send you any more letters. I won't stop loving you but I will stop telling you about it."

"I love your love. That sounds silly but, I mean it."

"Okay. Well. Here is the thing. I died. I am not sure how long ago it was, maybe twenty-five years ago, or more. And when I died I lost all memory of what happened to me before I died."

"Are you serious?"

"I am. I woke up on a gurney in a hospital in some desert town in Southern California. I was in a pretty sorry state, ragged beard, dirty like a vagrant, completely naked except for a white sheet over me. I was in a room with other dead bodies. I came to after having what was a very strange dream, or if not a dream something else, I guess they call it a near-death experience.

Though it was unlike any that I have ever read about. I heard the orderlies come. I was unable to move. I heard them speaking to each other above me, they said that I had shot enough heroin into myself to kill an elephant. One of them wanted to smoke a joint before tending to my corpse. They left and I managed to get down from the gurney and hide behind another one. When they came back, high as all hell, and saw my body missing, they made the decision to proceed with processing the corpse that was not there, rather than report that they had lost it."

"So, according to all records you are dead. The you that was you."

"Yes. I am dead. That me is dead."

"Wow. What happened next?"

"I found scrubs and made my way out of the hospital. It was the middle of night. I got some clothes by breaking into a thrift store. And then walked. I must have walked for hours, or even days. Eventually a woman in a truck picked me up and gave me a job on her farm picking kiwis."

"Kiwis?" she asked, laughing.

"Yes. And she gave me books to read. She was very kind. When the season was over she paid me and I was on my way."

"Where to?"

"Eventually New York City. After working odd jobs along the way. Hitching rides, jumping boxcars. The first thing that happened upon arriving in New York City was that a man gave me the keys to his bookstore. He needed an employee and I was in the right place at the right time. I worked in the bookstore for over ten years as the sole employee. It was a formative experience. Eventually I began to write and by some miracle got published."

"Your whole life has been a miracle, it seems."

"Yes. I took a breath and ventured, "The most miraculous part was meeting you. And I don't want to lose you."

CHAPTER 12

◆

I was in love with Minh.
I am in love with Minh. And, I think she is in love with me. I am in fact pretty sure of it. She says so. And I can read her thoughts by looking at her hands. One day, for instance, we were at Café Lux, she looked down at her hands, and her eyes were like planets, and I knew she was thinking about whether being with me was the right decision. So I leaned over and kissed her on the lips, I took her hand and told her that one of the reasons that I loved her so much was the way she analyzed a situation and based on an inherent wisdom and intuition, I knew she would always make the best decision for herself.

One night, in bed, she asked me what my fantasy was; I told her that my only fantasy was touch, to touch her and to make love to her. Simple, sensual pleasure. I told her that and said, "I know that's boring," and she said, "No, it's not," and she smiled and kissed my eyelids. She introduced a few other ideas to our lovemaking and it turned out I did quite enjoy them. There is the librarian fantasy. Where she wears her glasses, puts them down on the bridge of her nose (her very cute Vietnamese nose) and she is looking at books on the bookcase, taking some down, alphabetizing the books, and I come up to her from behind and I reach around her for a book while my other hand cups her breast. She says, "Can I help you find a book?" And I say, "No, thank you, I know where to look." And then I lift her skirt and pull down her panties, and I take out my erect cock and enter her from behind, and she makes these little sounds—

quiet, quiet because we are in a library.

I pump her slowly and then quicker and then quicker and then pull out. I turn her around and kiss her on the mouth. She puts her legs around my hips, and I lift her and take her into the bedroom. The library theme continues with her interjecting things like, "Why, sir, I hope I can help you find your books, you don't seem to be too interested in books." And I say, "I love books: Anaïs Nin, *Kama Sutra*, Apollinaire's *Les Onze Mille Verges ou les Amours d'un hospodar*, Marquis de Sade, Henry Miller, *Tropic of Cancer* and *The Rosy Crucifixion*, Colette, *Thérèse the Philosopher*, *Margot la Ravaudeuse*," and so on.

Yes, she undoubtedly loves me, inexplicably loves me, and won't be dissuaded from this. Well then, I figure that is part of my fortune, part of my invention. I have seen squalor and degradation. I have lived it. It is bad. When you are used to something, it is less bad. I never want to go back there again. What if I was dead, had died? I am not Lazarus. I am a man, or person, or something filled with life force now. It was what? Two lifetimes ago, or at least one lifetime ago. Depends on what age we are living in. And this entity who came out of dirt and vomit and then mud and rain and rags and fecal matter is clean and entirely new and entirely of my own creation. Like a truffle dog, I sniffed around for my identity and found it in bookstores and record stores; found my tools like the primate in *2001: A Space Odyssey*. Oh yes, in the cinema and at opera houses and concert halls. There, too, I found my identity, there it was languishing. Though I had nothing so much to write about aside from my own self-invention, I had stored memories, like all of us do. Stored memories from my descendants and antecedents. As Augustine says, time goes backwards, the future into the past, not the other way around. It helps to think this way.

CHAPTER 13

◆

Clouds like giant light bulbs flooded the sky over Manhattan. Minh wanted to go to a place called Ladurée, a fancy French bakery and tearoom in SoHo. I had to see the garden, she said. But it was raining, so we went inside, and sat amongst the little girls and their mothers. The little girls looked like American Girl dolls, all shiny white porcelain in Bonpoint dresses. The mothers looked as if their eyes had been replaced by marbles, as if they wished to be somewhere else, anywhere, so practiced at not showing it in their faces, their placid smiles. I wore a Ben Sherman suit that I had bought at Housing Works for sixty bucks. Looked like new. I didn't; the suit did. I put on a Gucci tie that I had bought on eBay for as much as the suit. After putting it on, I noticed that it had a few stains. I couldn't remember if I had caused the stains or if it might have come that way. It didn't matter because I didn't like the tie and told myself that I would never wear it again anyway. Minh wore a summer dress that went to her knees. She wore contacts and eyeliner that made those little wings which were fetching, alluring. As we sat at the table, in that turquoise room, filled with the screaming girls and the tired mothers, I felt older than my years, and she looked younger than hers.

I was thinking that, if anything, this demonstrates the impossibility of this relationship. I felt like a young man and maybe looked younger than my years, but I knew the world saw something different. More than that, as this scene demonstrated, there was something inherently impossible or untenable about the whole situation. She liked to romanticize the traditional roles of men and women, and she liked that I was so strong, as she put it. And I liked that she was feminine in how she presented herself. If this was traditional then so be it.

After lunch, as we left the restaurant, it started raining determinedly. I had no umbrella handy, so we ducked into the nearest shop, which happened to be Tiffany. "Let's look at the engagement rings. I need to find my size. Right?" Minh laughed and steered me to the proper counter. I gathered a glance of myself in the mirror. I looked like a sodden professor of linguistics or something: horn-rimmed glasses, wet hair that demonstrated the receding hairline, which was usually covered by crimson curls.

Minh tried on a few rings, each one lovely, to be sure. I hated it in there. "Four point five," the woman behind the counter said after guessing and measuring with the mandrel on her second try. Minh tried on a few. She ended up liking the most elegant one: thin band, good-sized diamond. It was also the most expensive one, the Tiffany True. She showed it to me. I smiled, or tried to smile. More of a wince. It wasn't my style, nor did I think it hers. Though things had been going well and I was finally in the chips, spending thirty thousand dollars on a ring seemed absolutely absurd to me. Upon seeing my expression, Minh's momentary glee faded quickly as she took off the ring and handed it back to the woman.

We stepped out of the store. It was still raining. "I'll go and buy an umbrella and come back," I said. Minh nodded. I walked through the streets of SoHo in a daze. What just happened? It was like Minh had been abducted and someone else put in her place. Someone who was more materialistic, more enraptured by the trappings of American materialism than the woman I had come to know and love. I finally found a bodega and bought a nice long umbrella. Not one of those collapsing kinds—and it was only eight dollars. That's when I really knew that things were not aligned between Minh and me. That I was so gleeful having to spend only eight dollars on an umbrella that looked and functioned exactly like one that might cost quite a bit more.

I walked in the rain, shielded from the falling water by my nice, black inexpensive umbrella. I got turned around and forgot which street Tiffany was on. Minh texted me, "Coming back?" emoji laugh/crying. "Soon," I wrote back. I found the block, and there she stood in the doorway, wearing her pretty summer dress with prints of white lambs, some upside down, which I had bought for her online from Brooks Brothers, with my new Brooks Brothers credit card. I also bought a few new suits to further and more effectively make my own transition to a different kind of New Yorker. Brooks Brothers was one thing; Tiffany is another. She smiled as I approached.

We walked down Prince Street, heading for Film Forum to watch a matinee of Buñuel's *The Discreet Charm of the Bourgeoisie*. "I had an idea for a short story while waiting for you. In it a couple visits Tiffany, where she tries on a few rings. After, as it is raining, he goes to get an umbrella and never comes back," she said, and then chuckled forcefully.
"I have a better idea. The man comes back with a ring that he had fashioned out of a paper clip and string, and it was more beautiful than the Tiffany ring."
Minh didn't like my ending to her story.

We both enjoyed Buñuel's taking down of the bourgeoisie in an endless farcical dinner scenario. After the film we grabbed dinner at Jack's Wife Freda. It was more tense between us than any other meal I ever had with her. We got home to Windsor Terrace and out of our wet clothes and into pajamas and the new fleece robes that I had bought for us from Brooklinen. I put on a record by Duke Ellington called *Blue Light*, very relaxing jazz. We drank tea and looked at magazines, her *The New Yorker* and me the *New York Review of Books*.

"Do you want to finish *Lost in Translation*?" she said
laconically.
"Okay."

We had started the film the night before. She had seen it a
few times. I had never seen it. She said, "Why don't you finish it.
I'm going to take a bath."

I was at the part where they were singing karaoke, New
Wave songs in a Tokyo bar. Obviously, something is happening
to the Scarlett Johansson character and the Bill Murray
character; perhaps they are falling in love.

Minh came out of the tub, her hair up in a towel. She sat
down next to me and watched the ending of the film, where
both characters go their separate ways, not attempting anything
more lasting romantically. Minh began to cry. I turned off the
television. I began to cry too. We exchanged a few words—the
gist being that perhaps her expectations and goals in a partner
didn't match mine. Of course, I didn't have any. The next
morning she packed up her few belongings and I gave her a ride
to her apartment. Ironically she had just moved to Park Slope to
be nearer to me, even though her commute to Columbia would
be two hours each day. I pulled up in front of her apartment,
went to kiss her as per usual, but pulled back. "Goodbye," I
said. "Goodbye.

CHAPTER 14

◆

What just happened? I asked myself as I lay in bed, Minh most definitely not next to me. She explained that yes, there was another side of her, not the side that loved opera and classical music and jazz and high literature, another side that I didn't know: the side that watched trashy TV shows about the Kardashians and liked to listen to nasty rap by Megan Thee Stallion, Janae, and wanted a nice engagement ring and a nice house and a rich husband to take care of her. The way she explained things to me sounded like poetry, a kind of lyric poetry. It made sense. And yet I was flummoxed. It wasn't that I had a false identity, or that I had died and come back to life with no recollection or awareness of my previous existence aside from the fact that I was a junkie. That didn't make her want to end things? It was that I wasn't the kind of man to buy her a Tiffany engagement ring.

Though why then did she seem to be so enamored of me, and why had she fallen in love with me—and I with her—so quickly and deeply-if those were her requirements for her ideal man? I was quite obviously not that man. Or was I? Maybe part of me was.

I went to return the fleece robes that I had just bought for us at Brooklinen in Williamsburg. The woman asked me why, and I told her that my girlfriend was allergic. "To cotton?" she asked dubiously. I nodded. We had trouble finding my receipt. It was not in my emails, and then I realized that I had used Minh's email as per the suggestion of the clerk on the day I purchased them. Since I had already made a purchase using my email getting the ten percent discount, I could use hers and get another ten percent off. "Please don't send the receipt of refund back to that email," I told the woman, who told me that she had to; it was store policy. "Can I just get a printed receipt?" I pleaded. She nodded. As I walked out of the store, I knew that she would send it to Minh regardless.

As I walked down Wythe Street, my phone chimed the cascading chime that was Minh's chime.

"Hey," she wrote.

"Please ignore any message you might have received from Brooklinen."

"Please call me."

I called her and explained about using her email to get the ten percent discount. "I'm sorry. I should have told you."

"Why did you return them?"

"They made me sad."

"That's what I want to talk to you about."

"The robes?"

"No. Well, yes. The robes. Us. I can't imagine my life without you."

"You can't."

"I can't and don't want to."

"Then what about . . ."

"I don't care about the ring or any of that. I love you. But maybe you don't want to be with me anymore."

"I do. Of course I do."

CHAPTER 15

◆

We were married. Happiest day of my life? Certainly, as far as I could remember. It was a simple ceremony on the roof of a restaurant on the Lower East Side. The restaurant served a fusion of Italian and Japanese. The people who worked there were very sweet to us. On the surface of it, at least in certain circumstances, we would receive certain looks, judgments from people as to the age difference. Sometimes I felt very self-conscious, stigmatized. The looks were filled with a kind of New York ridicule, the provincialism that came from the migration from the Midwest and other suburbs to the metropolis in search of wealth gained by making money off of money. It was weird because I felt perhaps twenty years younger than my age since it had only been twenty years since memory.

Minh had a few friends from Columbia, and I had a few friends from the bookstore, from the poetry group. The thing that really made the evening, the celebration, was that Jean-Claude had come in that day from Paris with his father, the legendary Sidney Bechet saxophone prodigy. Jean-Claude had his piano in tow, which he kept at a former girlfriend's place in the West Village. He would wheel it to Washington or Union Square. Said he made more money that way than in any club. They would make a thousand dollars a day. He wheeled his piano into the back room of the restaurant where we were having our private dinner. He and his father serenaded us and our group of friends between courses. "My wedding gift to you," he said. The best gift he gave to me was encouraging me not to give up with Minh.

When we got home, we were so exhausted from the celebration, though neither of us drank—someone gave Minh a glass of champagne; she took a couple of sips, and that was all—so exhausted were we, I wondered if we had it in us to consummate our union. I needn't have worried. As always, our passion burned, was seamless in the way we came together, the way we had no inhibitions with each other.

The morning after, I awoke to find myself alone. I rose and put on my pajamas and walked out of the bedroom. Minh was at the dining room table, writing in her notebook.

"Coffee?" I offered.

"Oh yes, please."

She never made coffee and would always wait for me. It was only a matter of flicking the switch, as I had loaded the Coffee Master with ground beans and water the night before. Always I did this. Just a matter of putting milk in the frother and pushing that button.

We had agreed on our second date that if we were to continue seeing each other, as we were both writers, anything that happened to us and between us was fair game. And so, though I could not be sure, I figured she was writing about the night before. I asked her, "What are you writing about?" I set the coffee down in front of her.

"Thank you," she said, looking up at me, waiting for a kiss which I delivered and then delivered again more passionately. "I started working on a YA novel about a superhero girl."

"Oh really. What kind of YA?"

"Mai is a superhero/supergirl. She helps, from an incredibly young age, to kick the marauding, massacring, napalm-dropping, Agent Orange–using nefarious Americans from her land, and in a most humiliating and embarrassing way. The helicopter birds unable to leave the ground are tilted into the water off the coast of Saigon. It is Mai who gives the final push. And then she does the most remarkable thing: she forgives the Americans. And the French and the Japanese and the Chinese too. And for this amazing act of nobility, she is given the magic powers of flight, of poetry, and of grand business acumen. She travels all over the world, learning the language of each country she visits so that she can instill in other young girls a sense of empowerment. She does this by showing them how to have fun and how to articulate their dreams.

She had already written the first chapter, which she showed to me. Always very open about her work, as I was—and am—about mine. After reading it I felt a pang of jealousy, in the way that writers get about another writer's work when it is good. And this was not only good, it was breathtaking. She sat at the dining table, drinking coffee as I sat across from her reading the pages. I put them down and got up.

"Where are you going?" she asked.

"To my typewriter to write. You have inspired me beyond measure. As always."

So I got to work on my new novel on that day. And, unlike Minh, I took directly from my own life . . . somewhat. It was the story of a man and a woman who met by chance at a restaurant on the Upper West Side. She instigates the conversation by asking the man, who is writing in his notebook, if he happens to be a writer. He admits that he is. She too is a writer. They begin a love affair, agreeing that anything that happens to them is fair game. Each one ends up writing about their love from the other's perspective. And this act of projecting, of romantic empathy is the thing that allows for their love to flourish. My goal: to write a romantic novel about a cohesive and loving relationship. The tension is between the lovers and the outside world.

CHAPTER 16

◆

In the dream was someone like Minh, though not her. She was not crying; in fact, her face was stone. That is when I realized that she was not Minh. In fact, she looked almost nothing like Minh. She had blue eyes and dark blonde hair. Glaring at me in disgust, she told me to look at myself in the mirror. And on the door to a bedroom was a full-length mirror. I looked at myself, and it was I, now quickly transformed into a vagabond: wearing rags, unkempt, unclean, red splotches on my face. And then quickly transformed back into another me: more clean, a pencil mustache, and slicked-back hair like Rudy Valentino. She said she was leaving. She held a baby in her arms.

"I'm leaving you. I don't love you."

"How? Why? What have I done?"

"You've done nothing. I just don't love you."

"When? Where?"

"I love someone else, and we are moving to Europe."

"But what about my child?"

"This is not your child. Not anymore."

And I turned into a wolf and wailed.

"Wake up, wake up," Minh said, cradling me in her arms, kissing my forehead.

Two days later, I got the proofs for my latest novel. Another story of suburban life and how the decay of the traditional infrastructure of the family unit affects the children detrimentally. To the extent that the children assume the roles of the arbiters of morality. It was also a murder mystery. A child witnesses a murder but does not feel empowered to reveal his account to the adult authorities. The cover was a painting of a young boy with the inner part of his face painted black. It was jarring, though it was quite beautiful. I showed it to Minh. "What do you think?" She looked at it. "I don't like it. I mean, it is a good painting, but I don't think it is right for your novel." I didn't think so either, but I didn't have a say over the cover art—not in my contract, anyway.

"Let's see the author's photo." She opened the back of the book, and on the overleaf was a photo of me. It was the me of now, taken by my friend Eugene in a café in SoHo. "Your eyes are sad, but you are very handsome," she said.

And so what exactly am I? Was I nothing before, and now, because I am fully conscious of my place, am I something? I see the world through my subjective consciousness, but the world only exists as I see it, if not for my consciousness of the world the world would not exist, therefore mine is obviously an objective perspective. I see Minh as this person who is fundamentally and quite literally angelic in my perceptions, of the world, and in the language that is in my supply. But what do I know of her or of the world, except for what I can see and hear and smell and touch and absorb through skin and hair and eyes and eyelashes?

It is a thin line. It is a thin line for me. I don't know what is fiction and what is not. My subconscious is subterfuge. I draw from it to write stories, short- and long-form. But I have no way of knowing whether the stories are true or not. Stories of childhood in Southern California, stories of adolescent suburban drug addiction, stories of an early marriage, of children, of death and life regained. I have no way of knowing how much of it is true. Sometimes I think that I might hire a private detective, now that I can afford one. But perhaps it is better this way. Not to know.

Minh came over one night. Before we were married. She had a dozen yellow roses. She wore a red dress and had her hair drawn back. She looked older, almost severe, yet very alluring. She asked me if I would like to read the first chapter of her

new novel. I said of course I did. She made tea and put the
roses in a vase while I read the twenty or so pages. It was the
story of a young woman and her lover, who was at least twice
her age. They were in Paris, shacked up in an apartment in
the Latin Quarter. They spent the days wandering the streets
of the 4th arrondissement, the Île Saint-Louis, preferring the
boulevards and side streets to the museums. And at night, all
night, making love. Discovering each other, yet more than that,
discovering their own bodies as if they were newborn. As if
they had been dropped entirely whole from another dimension.
Bodies, mysterious until the touch of another whose touch was
stimulating, whose thoughts were stimulating, whose looks and
expressions were stimulating. Enjoying scientific discussions
in the morning on the nature of love and beauty. And the
difference between solitude and loneliness, of desire and longing
and self-sufficiency. Discussions of a phantom power, of a
universe that made more sense than was nonsensical.

"I wrote that before we met. Isn't that amazing?"

PART TWO

CHAPTER 17

◆

A couple years later, as we sat on the porch of the house we lived in in Ditmas Park, the house that we purchased as a result of selling books, we read the Sunday *New York Times* in the light of a summer morning. Coffee in off-white, light blue speckled ceramic mugs sat on a tray next to the near-empty insulated stainless steel French press; crumbs from cinnamon buns made by Minh lay desolate on a vintage white and blue Japanese plate with a peacock etched in intricate gilt detailing, part of a collection given to us by Minh's mother as a wedding gift. Minh was reading the Book Review, and I was reading the Week in Review. I couldn't help but stop to reflect how incredible all of this was. How so much of my life was blank. Literally no account. I hired a private detective, in fact a team of them, to find out who I was; they came up empty. It was actually Minh who suggested it. Not that she was overwhelmingly curious; she just thought, with the notoriety I was receiving, it might make sense to get in front of anything. But there was nothing they could find. And so here we were, living our best life.

I looked over to her. She had stopped reading. She had her legs crossed and eyes closed in meditation. She sometimes did this without any announcement, just crossed up that way for five, ten, fifteen minutes, and I knew, of course, not to disturb her. I envied her this ability. I tried to emulate her but could never stop my mind from racing. Her hair had grown quite long. It hung down to her elbows, the dark brown hair with faint traces of auburn. She looked so peaceful, and that peacefulness found its way toward me. It was almost as good as meditating myself.

I looked up and there was a young woman standing on our lawn. She wore a yellow summer dress with daisies that resembled the daisies that stood to the side of her in our garden. Her hair was red, and her face had many freckles. She looked to be in her late teens. She said, "Hello. Sorry to disturb you but I am pretty sure that I am your daughter."

"Is that so?" I asked, setting down my coffee mug. She nodded. I motioned for her to come up to us. "You don't seem surprised," she said as she walked forward. I stood and offered her my chair. Minh opened her eyes. She tilted her head as she took in the girl. "Who is this?" she asked, motioning with her thumb. "She says she thinks that perhaps she is my daughter." Minh picked up her glasses, which were by the French press on the tray. She put them on. She brushed back her hair and looked at the girl. "You don't say."

"I have been curious about who my actual father is for a long time. On my eighteenth birthday, which I celebrated at a Winchell's doughnut shop all alone, I picked up a *Los Angeles Times* with a review of the show based on your book, *Modern Instances*. It mentioned the writer being very reclusive, and that there was not much information about him except that he was born in Southern California, worked in a bookstore for years, and guarded his privacy. And there was a photo of you. And your face, filled with freckles."

But there was that whole part that came before my awakening. Maybe two decades of life. Where it appears I was somebody, could have been somebody who had been with a woman and had procreated. Had made this young woman who stood before me on my lawn in Ditmas Park. Her hair red and face freckled much like mine. So articulate were her words, so conclusive. She was quite certain I was her father. When she saw the photo of me in the newspaper accompanying a review of my latest book, she knew that there was a connection, yet she couldn't know how. When she showed the article and the photo to her mother, it was her mother's befuddled expression that gave her certainty. The mother said, almost to herself, "I know this man."

"What's your name?"

"My name is Dorothy."

"Dorothy, this is my wife, Minh."

"I know. I have read all of your books."

"You have? Well, thank you."

"Thank you. That is also how I knew."

"Knew what?" I said, more curious than astonished.

"Knew that you were my father. I knew that you had been married. That was in the article. And that you were married to a novelist. Minh. So I went to the library and checked out all three of your novels. I have read all of Dad's books and now yours too. Do you mind if I call you Dad?"

"I don't mind. But how can you be so sure? Sounds like a lot of circumstantial evidence."

"And intuition. Which is better than circumstantial evidence," Minh said. "Would you like a coffee, or perhaps an Arnold Palmer?" And Minh motioned for Dorothy to come up to the porch where we were sitting.

"What's an Arnold Palmer?"

Minh was looking intently at Dorothy as she gently swung back and forth on the swing attached to the roof of the porch. Dorothy's yellow dress looked lovely against the yellow of the painted swing. "You do bear a resemblance, and not because you are both gingers. It's your eyes, the way they are a little more open than most people keep them. And your mouth, that same half-smirk, like you both are in on some kind of inside joke. I can't say for certain, yet I would wager to guess that Dorothy knows of what she speaks."

I looked at her. Maybe eighteen, nineteen years old, give or take. She looked happy. So very happy. It reminded me of how happy I was. That very morning, waking up, having been awakened by the dog shifting position at my feet and opening my eyes and seeing Minh, so pretty and peaceful, her eyelids closed tightly, rapid eye movements, some dreams, and her chuckling in her sleep, which was something that happened often.

I thought about how fortunate I was. I didn't even have that usual pang of anxiety that accompanies awareness of that good fortune. As if, at any minute, it could be taken away. I kissed Minh on the cheek. Didn't wake her. I got up, called for the dog. Took him out to the yard, where he peed and then had a poop, which happened every morning just like that. That poop always amazed me because every night before going to bed Minh and I would take Humphrey out for a stroll up Argyle Street, down and around Rugby, and then back up Argyle to our house. Where he did his business. Where did that morning poo come from since he hadn't eaten anything since five o'clock the evening before? Another mystery of life.

As is my usual routine, I come in and feed Humphrey his morning meal. I turn on the lovely Technivorm Moccamaster, which I had loaded the night before, to percolate the coffee, put milk into the Bodum milk frother, press the red button, and wait for all of that to take place. By then, Minh is up and stirring in the bedroom. I bring in two cups of coffee, with some raw sugar. And what a fortunate life, and what a fortunate morning. All of the news in the newspaper, either bad or good, is of less consequence in the midst of all of this. But it does seem that since I met Minh everything has gotten better. Not just my life, my happiness, but the conditions of the world.

Dorothy had no place to stay. She had a pink cardboard suitcase and blue canvas satchel, a fedora hat that sat atop a bushy mound of red hair. She wore cat eye glasses that resembled Minh's and had black nail polish on her fingernails and red on her toenails, which you could see through the toe holes of her beaten Birkenstocks. She might be mistaken for a hippie, even though her look was more fifties than sixties. She chewed gum incessantly. The only time she wasn't chewing gum was when she took out the old piece to put in a new piece of Wrigley's spearmint. And when she was eating. Eating dinner with Minh and me.

I had broiled three salmon steaks and steamed some rice

and vegetables. I did most of the cooking and most of the dishes. It was not that Minh wasn't willing; I just knew that she would rather not do the cooking and the cleaning, and I didn't mind it. I really didn't. "Do you eat fish?" I asked Dorothy as I put down the platter of salmon. "I do," she said. "I'm a pescatarian." She looked at me and then at Minh and started laughing. "Actually, I'm a complete omnivore."

"You know," Dorothy said while ravenously destroying a whole steak of salmon, "I think I discovered a lot of things about you. A lot of things that you might not even know." On the porch I had told Dorothy that I had forgotten—or not forgotten—had wiped from my memory most of all the years before I died. "Since you can't recall anything that happened to you before you died, maybe you might find it interesting to hear what I have found out. Unless you don't want to know. You might not want to know. I mean you might feel more comfortable not knowing."

"But if it is something that it is better that I know . . . I don't know. What do you think, Minh?"

Minh took a sip of her Arnold Palmer, set it down on the table in our dining room. A long pine table that I had made, just like everything; all of the furniture in the house I had made. All of it unstained pine or birch plywood. She said, "Maybe you should know."

Minh reached out for my hand, took hold of it, gave it a little squeeze, looked me in the eye, turned to Dorothy, and said, "Dorothy, I find it very interesting that you have come to us at this time. I don't mean to sound suspicious, and I am not. I just find it curious. You know, it is funny, even my meeting Geronimo when I did, and that we were both in some ways at the exact same age—of our development, that is. He had only been cognizant for some twenty-six years, and I about the same. And that we were both writers and both preferred to be alone most of the time. When we met, actually, it was I who broke the ice. I don't think he would ever have done so. Still, I did, and it seems like we were always very comfortable with each other. And both of us usually were not so with others. I look at you, and it is true you physically resemble him. This cannot be denied, but you are a different specimen, a different kind of human being. I have never seen one quite like you before, and so I am very curious."

"Oh, I get it. You think that I am perhaps pulling a grift."

"Pulling a grift? Oh no. I don't think so. I believe you are sincere. I also believe that you are correct. I don't know how, I just sense it. You are his daughter."

At this point, the way Minh was speaking, it was like a song she was singing, like an aria from one of the operas we had seen at the Met, and it had lulled me away from the content of what she said. But now I was fully listening. She was talking about me, even though it seemed as if she and Dorothy were speaking about someone else. "When I tell you all of what I know, then you will be certain."

CHAPTER 18

◆

Later that night in bed, I stroked Minh's hair as she read Virginia Woolf's *Mrs. Dalloway*. She looked so charming even though she was disquieted. I was not. None of it mattered to me. None of what Dorothy brought did I find threatening. "I am not threatened," Minh said, reading my thoughts. "How could I be threatened by anything that young woman might have up her sleeve? She is not a magician." She set down the book in the space between us. I picked it up and looked at the cover. A drawing of a vase of flowers, a line drawing. I looked at the back cover to see the artist. Linda Vang. What a coincidence: the same last name as Minh and me. When Minh and I got married, we both took each other's names because we had the same last name. Although my Vang I purchased for five hundred dollars on the new identity black market, so that I could have an identity, so that I could have a passport and credit cards and credit, et cetera.

"This is one of the few of Virginia's I haven't read," I said.

"I wrote my thesis on it. I am rereading it again. You can have it after I get done with it. I am almost done."

She snuggled up close to me. Then she got on top of me, took off my black horn-rimmed glasses, and set them down on the nightstand that I had built out of three-quarter-inch birch plywood. She kissed me. I reached up and put my left hand on her right breast, hugged it with my hand and then squeezed her nipple. She made a sound that I could only compare to the sound of air being released from the mouth of a sleeping baby when it is happy and secure in its swaddling blanket. I put my ear to her cheek. Her flesh was cool and warm.

About a half hour later, after we had made each other happy, we concluded with a joke: "Why, Mrs. Dalloway, you take my breath away."

"Why, Mr. Walsh. Please call me Clarissa."

As I was getting my pants on, Minh said to me, "I know you are more concerned than you let on, or maybe you are not. Still, don't worry. We can handle anything."

Someone was screaming, high-pitched, "Oh my god! Oh my god!" I went to the window of our bedroom, which was on the second floor that overlooked the backyard. At least it sounded like it was coming from the backyard. I saw Dorothy down there, again exclaiming, "Oh my god! Oh my god!"

We walked downstairs, through the kitchen, and out onto the backyard. "Jesus Christ!" She turned around, her eyes all lit up and her mouth agape. "What the hell are those?" We walked to her. Minh touched her arm. "Those are fireflies. You've never seen them. They don't occur on the West Coast."

"Fireflies. Of course. I have read about them in books. There are so many." It was true, this was one of those nights of peak fireflies, a wall of firefly light. You take things for granted, yet I had the same reaction when I first encountered fireflies. I had been in New York City for almost a year, and one night, after closing the bookstore, I went for a long walk. A very long walk north, to the top of Manhattan, the reservoir in Central Park, and all along the way I encountered their flickering. I looked at the luminescent flickering light and then up at the city lights, and the syllogism of nature and urbanity, pretty urbanity, made a profound impact on me. And gave me that feeling, that sense of well-being, that sense that one is in the right place at the right time.

Dorothy's face seemed luminescent in the light of the hovering insects. She began to laugh, and this made Minh and me laugh as well. Once Minh starts laughing, really laughing, she can't stop, and it is such a joyous thing. And Dorothy, seeing and hearing Minh laughing, opened her eyes and mouth wider and in turn lost control. It was as joyous a moment as I had ever experienced.

CHAPTER 19

◆

Dorothy was saturnine after the excitement of the fireflies, after the exuberance of the fireflies. We went back inside, to the living room. Minh sat arms akimbo on the chaise lounge. Dorothy sat without bones ("sat without bones"??) on the sofa. I put on a Paul Bley record: his recording of his wife Carla's composition of a song called "Ida Lupino." Minh studied Dorothy as if she were a painting by Modigliani. Then she picked up Virginia's *Mrs. Dalloway*, which she had retrieved from upstairs, and began to read. I brought around fresh Arnold Palmers for everyone and sat down on the floor, my back to the chaise where Minh sat. I picked up a volume of Sartre that sat on the coffee table.

"Being is. Being is itself. Being is what it is," I said. Minh looked up from *Mrs. Dalloway*. "Reading Sartre again?" Dorothy moved her head, which had been stuck in the same position for a few minutes. She looked at me and smiled. "What does it mean?" I shrugged. Minh said, "I think that it means, and what Sartre is saying, is that being is irrefutable, and the contemplation of consciousness forms our identity, is who we are, is what it is."

"Yes, but what about when we are dead?" Dorothy said morosely.

"I was reading about this the other day in Hannah Arendt's book on Saint Augustine. She talks about Augustine's theory of the double negative. The two distinct phases or jumps of our existence, of our being. The stage of NOT YET and then the NO MORE. A person emerging from the not yet stage goes

in search for their own being. There is a commonality between
Sartre and Augustine in many ways."

"Yes, but what about the no more?"

I picked up the copy of *Love and Saint Augustine* on the
coffee table. "Love is itself our death to the world, and our
life with God. For if it is death when the soul leaves the body,
how is it not death when our love goes forth from the world?
Therefore, love is as strong as death."

Dorothy asked, "You actually died. Did your soul leave your
body? Did you get a new soul when you were resurrected?"

"How do you know for certain that I died?"

"It just figures. I probably know more about you than
you know."

"So go on. I want to know. I want to know all about me," I
said, rising and then sitting down properly on the sofa, near but
not next to Dorothy.

"I will tell you what I know, and like I said, I think I know
a lot. You were born in Long Beach, California, in 1979. August
9th, to be exact. Your father sold insurance, and your mother
was a nurse. Both died in a car crash when you were ten years
old. At that time, you went to live with your grandparents in
Downey. You were a good kid: no police record. In the local
newspaper it said you made Eagle Scout and were awarded
for civic work you did as a Boy Scout. You did well in school
and got a scholarship to UCLA in the English department.
You have always been a writer. After college you got a job at a
newspaper. I have seen photos of you at that time: long beard,
shaggy hair, no glasses. You looked like a regular bohemian.
You met Mom, my mother, at that time. Candace. Candace
came from a very wealthy background. Unlike you. Your people
are from the lower half of the middle class, hers from the
uppermost part. Candace's lineage is Mayflower straight down
the line. Yours are immigrants, both Eastern Europe, on your
father's part, and Mexico, on your mother's. Nevertheless, you
met and, I suppose, fell in love, because you got married. I was
born shortly after. And either you were fired or you quit the
newspaper. Mother opened a gallery in Santa Monica. And so

you took care of me."

"When I was about one year old, Mom fell in love with one of her artists, a very famous and successful one. So, she took me and left you. Apparently this was too much for you. This and whatever else, so you lost your job and basically became a drunk and a drug addict. You were arrested a few times on vagrancy and possession charges. You were about to be put away for a long time. You had two strikes, and the third strike meant a practical life sentence, or in your case, a death sentence. You died on March 26th, 1993. Drug overdose. Heroin. Your body was taken to Potter's Field, and you were dumped there. All of these things are a matter of public record. Not terribly hard to find out once I learned your real name."

"What is it?" Minh asked.

"What is what?" Dorothy replied.

"My real name," I said.

"Your real name is Gerald Clinton Hopson."

"You know," Minh said, rising, straightening her dress and walking over to the record player, "Before you came here, there was no past in this house." She flipped the record over and put the needle down. Paul Bley started playing again. "At least, none that mattered. None that we spent any time talking about."

"You're living in a fantasy. I am not saying that is a bad thing. Yet these things, these things that happened, they are real. And they are going to find you, Dad. It is better you know."

"I don't care one way or another. In fact, I am curious. The thing is, you're calling me Dad. And it is kind of funny. I am not your dad. Even if I am, biologically. Your dad is the man who raised you. The painter who your mom left me for."

"Then you remember?"

"No, you just told me."

"He didn't raise me."

"He left?"

"No, he died. Maybe murdered. Shortly before you died."

"Oh."

"In fact, you were the main suspect. But then you died, and

since he was not a U.S. citizen, his family came for his body, the case was dropped."

"How did he die?" Minh asked as she sat down next to me, taking hold of my hand.

"He fell or was pushed from a very tall ladder."

"You say you found out about me. How did you do that?"

"Newspaper articles, mostly. I have it all in my suitcase. I can show you."

"That's okay," I said, accepting all that she said.

"So, what are you doing here? Just to confront Geronimo with what you know?"

"No. I am not trying to be confrontational. I am trying to help. The thing is, I love you. I know that. Because you are my dad. I know you are, and solely because of that, I love you. But then I love who you are as well. You're an incredible person and a great writer." Taking pause to regroup, Dorothy added, "And I love you too, Minh. I know your story, too. You came to the U.S. and you came by yourself when you were only fourteen. You got into a prestigious boarding school and then Ivy League and then Columbia, and you have published three best-selling novels. I spent my whole childhood reading books and watching movies. You two are the kind of people that I read about, watched, and wanted to be."

"So, that is why you are here? Because you love us?" I asked.

"That, and I got a film scholarship to NYU. I want to be a filmmaker."

I looked at Minh. What was her reaction to all of this? She looked quite serious but then began to chuckle. "Well, then."

CHAPTER 20

◆

The phone rang. I answered it. It was a woman asking for Dorothy. The voice sounded familiar. "Dorothy, it is for you." Dorothy got up and I handed her the phone.

"Hello? Oh hi, Mom."

Minh shook her head and picked up *Mrs. Dalloway* and began to read. She had this incredible talent for being able to tune out noise and the world when she read. I could be calling her name, and if she was especially immersed in a book, she couldn't or wouldn't hear me. Now I listened.

"Yeah, I am good. I am staying with my friends in Brooklyn. I'm not sure. I'll let you know. Okay, I love you." She hung up the phone and sat back down.

"That was your mother?" I asked her.

"Yep."

"Does she know about all of this? Does she think that I am alive?"

"No. She doesn't know, and I never let on about any of it."

"That's good, I guess."

"So, school starts in a couple weeks. I was wondering, and you can say no. You can totally say no, but . . ."

"Yes," Minh said, without lifting her head from the book. "You can stay here."

CHAPTER 21

◆

The city changes and is never the same. If you stand in the same spot on the same corner, stand and wait, and the people, many people, some walk in a certain way, the same way, the city walk, one arm with broad strokes chopping at the air, you see that walk often. Or the hunched-over slouch forward, or the look when walking, staring straight ahead; different people have the same style of walking. I have been told that my walk is noticeable. I have been told that my walk is a sort of bouncing down the street. As I put my foot down flat and then rotate to the ball of the foot, causing the bounce. I have been told that I can be detected a block away because of my bounce. But the city changes, the buildings, the businesses, the vehicles, the clothing styles to a lesser extent, the people. Not the way we walk though.

Every day is different, every day something momentous happens. The days pass, and I look in the mirror and I don't seem to age. It is fantastic. I guess that's why the age gap between Minh and me not only does not seem to register to me, it does not seem to get much notice from the people we encounter. Not even Dorothy. She did not mention it. There is a kinship between her and Minh. We are all three similar in a core way. We are all orphans, to a certain extent. Of course, Minh and Dorothy have parents. But they have pretty much raised themselves. I had—or have—parents, but I have pretty much raised myself. Or, I consider the city to be my parent.

The days passed, summer ended, and Dorothy went to school during the week. She made friends. Though she was somewhat mysterious about them, she seemed glad of it, of making acquaintances. Sometimes she came home late in the morning and we would have a brief chat over coffee before she was off again. Then Minh and I have our coffee and chat and read, or look at magazines before we head off to our respective studies to work on the manuscripts in progress. Reconvene for lunch. And either go back to work or decide to go and see a movie or an exhibition at a museum or gallery, and then sometimes grab dinner somewhere in Manhattan. Or just come home, and I would make a meal. And of course, we would go to see an opera once or twice a month. After lunch, I would put the dog Humphrey in the basket of my bike and go for a long ride through Ditmas Park and Midwood, and then to the Kensington dog run, where Humphrey likes to romp for roughly forty-five minutes. And then back to work for a spell.

It was a good life. Sedate and prosperous. Neither one of us was willing to go on arduous book tours, though we had both been told that this would hamper sales. Yet sales were fine. Both our works have been licensed to the streaming services for films or series. We take trips to Paris or London or Rome or Naples, purely for leisure. Sometimes we talked about having a baby, or her having a baby. But it never seemed to be something we are particularly invested in. And now Dorothy had joined us, and for how long nobody seemed to be curious or even care about knowing. One day at a time. And the mystery—the ominous warning from Dorothy to me, the secrets of my past—a sort of ticking time bomb. Yet, after the first disclosure, that also subsided. That is, until she mentioned that her mother was coming to visit.

"Don't worry. She is staying in the city and I will meet her for dinner or lunch or whatever. She is only staying a few days."

"What does she do?" I asked, feeling a tremendous anxiety welling up in my throat, which strangled my words.

"She still owns the gallery. Though she doesn't need to work. She has millions from the sale of my stepdad's works."

"You call him your stepdad, but you were still an infant when he was killed," Minh said, sipping her coffee.

"Well, that's what he was."

"No matter," Minh replied.

Dorothy went off to school, Minh to her office, and I got on my bike and went for a ride around Prospect Park. I pedaled faster and faster. The men in their tight fluorescent spandex outfits sped past me. Can I recall this woman? What is she? What does she look like? What did she look like? I was in love with her; this I knew. Like a disease I was in love with her. And she betrayed me. She took my daughter and left me for a successful painter from Bolivia. But was I capable of killing someone? Of killing this man? I felt at that moment, as I had gotten myself pretty worked up, that the person that I was, the nihilist who took all of those drugs and killed himself with them—well, if he killed himself that way then it made sense that he was capable of killing someone else, especially the man who caused tragedy and trauma to befall him.

Still, the man that I was presently, *that* man—if I dug deep down into my psyche—into that man, it didn't seem possible, or it was not conceivable, that he could murder. But was I both men, or just the one man divided into two parts or more?

CHAPTER 22

◆

Minh was wearing the black negligée that I had bought for her in Paris, together with her cat eye glasses; she had the authentic look of a cartoon vixen. I had to try not to laugh. She commanded me to remove my clothing, which I did. She shoved me on the bed. She got on her knees, crawled between my legs. She grimaced like a lioness and bit my inner thigh. Not gently—hard—hard enough to puncture skin.

After we made love, lying astride me, she said, "When are you going to put an end to this?"

"What do you mean?"

"This threat."

"Is that why you bit me?"

She didn't say anything. I got up, put on my robe; I sat back down at the edge of the bed. "You mean Dorothy living here?"

"Yes. But more than that. I don't feel good about her and about the whole situation. She is out to destroy you or blackmail you or something."

"I am not so sure. And she is my daughter. That, though confusing, is having an impact on my psyche."

"And her mother, your ex, is coming. Frankly, I am alarmed."

"What do you suggest?"

"Let's flee."

"What?"

"Let's leave. Let's get the fuck out of here. Pack up the house, shutter it, and move to France. For at least a while.

Maybe permanently."

The phone rang. I reached over to the night table and picked up the receiver. It was my publisher. I mouthed "Alice" to Minh. She shrugged her shoulders, got out of bed, put on a sun dress, and walked out of the room.

I hadn't actually gotten anywhere with the novel. Not since Dorothy had come into my life. The novel itself wasn't making a whole lot of sense to me. Actually, I had no idea what was going to happen. I had no blueprint, no written arc, no 3x5 cards with character analysis. No graphs or micrographs of the action and the culmination. None of the things that I had done in the past. I thought that this time I would just sit down and write, sit down and write at least a page a day. Write at least a page a day, and in one year, in 365 days, I would have the rough draft. And if I missed a day here and there, I would do an extra page or two here and there. I knew that once I got at least halfway through there would be momentum to move things along. Yet for now, just a page a day. A page a day. Was that asking too much? Apparently it was, because I would go some time, a day or two or three days without a page. And so my rhythm was herky-jerky. I had characters, and they were taking form, they were becoming independent, organic, holistic beings, entities. They were beginning to speak to me, they were finding their voices. They were pushing back. Back against me. Telling me that they didn't like where I was taking their characters. One character in particular, the wife of the protagonist, just up and left. Said she couldn't take it anymore. And when asked when she would be coming back, she just shrugged. Shrugged and left.

I didn't know where it was going. I was more concerned with where my life was going. What all of this meant. If Dorothy was making a veiled threat, to expose me as a murderer and to see my facade, and in turn my whole life, come crumbling down, why didn't she just do it? That is because, I thought, why would she? If I was her father, why would she want to hurt me? Why wouldn't she want to protect me? But if she was not my daughter, then I could see the blackmail angle. But she was my daughter.

I went for a bike ride. When I got back I made turkey sandwiches for Minh and myself. Minh came downstairs carrying her vintage cherry-red Samsonite luggage. She wore a black miniskirt, black top with white Peter Pan collar, the pearl necklace and earrings that I had given her. And a vintage over-the-shoulder Pan-Am bag. She was leaving because of Dorothy. But mostly because Dorothy's mom, my ex-wife, my widow, was coming. Not because she was jealous or felt threatened. Not threatened by her being my ex. Maybe threatened in the sense that she felt that only bad things would happen. I told her that I was not going to leave. I was not going to go to France. I was staying and I was not afraid. She called me stupid. But not in a mean way. She was never mean. And she was right.

We embraced. We hugged. We kissed. We didn't say anything. Her phone buzzed. She looked at it, put it in her bag, and smiled at me. "Okay, you get things sorted out. I believe in your judgment and ability to handle things. I just need a break."

"You're going to Paris?"

"No, Hanoi. To see my family and then spend some time at the beach in Da Nang."

"That is good. Give them my love."

"I will."

CHAPTER 23

◆

I took out a Mexican Coke, poured it into a glass with a couple of cubes of ice, took the Coke to the front porch and sat down. The front porch where Minh and I had first seen Dorothy. When would I see Minh next? Already I was missing her, and she had only been gone for five minutes. On the other hand, I was unfathomably pleased that I had a daughter and that my daughter was Dorothy. I liked her. She was smart, funny, and quirky. And she never said what you might expect. I always enjoy people like that. On the other hand I was ambivalently nervous and excited to see her mother.

I was only excited because I was curious. Curiosity motivated me. More than anything. I had been curious about Minh. I wanted to know about her. Why was she attracted to me? I felt that I could not answer this question sufficiently. I am not handsome. Not in a classical way. Not by modern standards. My unkempt graying red hair is full and sprawling. Slightly pudgy with disproportionately long arms and short fingers. My angular nose that the tortoise shell horn-rimmed glasses rested on. For so long I had a paper clip holding one of the arms in place, until I decided, when I had money, to go to Optical 88 on Mott Street. They fixed the glasses and also gave me a new prescription, since the one I had was over ten years old. It was amazing how clear the world became after that. Maybe no surprise, or maybe not a coincidence, that my writing had more clarity after the new prescription.

But Minh was an enigma. If I said that Dorothy always

said what you might not expect, Minh took that concept even further, not only saying what was least expected or what was surprising, then following her declaration with a short, poetically precise extrapolation. More than that, the thing that made me curious about Minh was me. What was it about her that gave me courage, that filled my heart in a way that I could never remember feeling before? Yes, my heart. That organ in my chest that got giddy when I was with her and that was throbbing with anxiety now that she was gone.

This chapter, this thing that had happened, had to be solved. My own enigma had to be solved. And I was curious. Curious as to who I was before. I was curious as to what had happened that had caused me to turn to drugs and alcohol to numb and then eventually end my life, if only temporarily. And I was curious as to whether or not I had killed the painter—my cuckold, Dorothy's stepfather, and my ex-wife's husband.

I went to the backyard and took a trampoline from the old carriage house that was Minh's painting studio and storage for sundry things. Rolling out the trampoline, I set down its legs, and let it drop. About eight feet wide in circumference and three feet off the ground. I had bought it at a yard sale a few houses down. Fifty bucks—seemed like a good way to burn off some steam, and a fun way at that. But the truth was it never got used much, and the grass underneath it grew disproportionately and then turned brown. Not wanting to get rid of it, with Minh's permission I put it in the carriage house.

I was bouncing up and down for five, ten, fifteen minutes. And then I lost track of time. It was a warm September day. The sky was blue and clear and reminded me of another day. I saw Dorothy enter the backyard. Blue dress, black felt hat, red hair. "Hey! That looks like fun. Can I come up too?" She was by my side as we bounced up and down in sync. "I didn't know you had a trampoline. I used to be in gymnastics at school. I love these things. Something about the act of bouncing up and down that grounds one, in a funny way."

Is that what I was looking for? To be grounded? No. The opposite. Still. I saw what she meant. My life was all of a sudden completely unsettled and yet it was probably a good thing. A good opportunity to take inventory of what was most important. Of how time is finite, and how the things that we love and cherish cannot be taken for granted, because when that happens, that's when we lose them. Dorothy, in a singsong voice, said, "We shall see one another again and not recognize one another, even if we have to be friends."

"What?"

"We shall see one another again and not recognize one another, even if we have to be friends."

"What is that?"

"Francis Picabia."

"Oh."

"Mother is coming."

"What, when?"

"Now."

I bounced right off the trampoline, banged my head on a rock, and passed out.

CHAPTER 24

◆

Looking up, I saw Dorothy, her long red hair hanging down. She had a crooked smile, scrunched up nose, and a halo. Next to her was another face, the face of a woman. She also wore a halo. She looked disconcerted. We engaged in eye contact. Deep, reset, reconnoitered eye contact. Her long dyed black hair, which mirrored and contrasted Dorothy's, as did her face, minus the smile, but the same bright eyes.

"Are you alright? Should we call an ambulance?"

"No, that's quite alright."

"This is my mother, Shirley," Dorothy said. "And this is Geronimo."

"So I gathered," Shirley said as she reached down her hand to give me a lift up. A bit wobbly, I made it over to the picnic table and sat down on one of the teak chairs. We sat quietly for a minute or two, allowing me to regain my equilibrium.

"So you're Geronimo. I want to thank you for putting Dorothy up. When she told me she found a room for rent on Craigslist, I was a bit doubtful. This is such a nice neighborhood, and you are quite a reputable writer. Well, it seems good. And where is Minh? I would love to meet her." She spoke with a twang, Southern California mixed with something more abrasive. And though her demeanor was pleasant, there was a shocking sadness to her.

Once I regained my balance, I suggested that I go to the store and get some ground beef for burgers. There was a decent market only a few blocks away. I got on my bike and rode over.

In the kitchen I chopped garlic and red onion and massaged these, along with spices and sea salt, into the meat in a large ceramic bowl bought from Crate & Barrel only a few months earlier. I found that I was quite enjoying being domesticated. Crate & Barrel offers a credit card, and you take it and you purchase the items while receiving an introductory twenty percent discount. You get home and log into your computer and set up your account and pay the thing off immediately. That was what Minh told me: don't let debt accumulate on those cards; otherwise your introductory discount and any savings will go right down the toilet.

When the coals were nice and gray, I put the patties on the grill. Dorothy and Shirley sat at the teak picnic table, drinking lemonade and occasionally looking at me and smiling. I put the cooked patties on a platter on the table with a bag of buns and cut tomatoes from the garden—Minh's tomatoes—along with lettuce and assorted condiments. Eight patties in all. Dorothy had three, Shirley two, and I had one. Their appetites were quite impressive. So unbridled their consumption of the burgers that conversation ceased. Until they were noshing on dill pickle spears. Shirley said, "It is funny. I had read one of your books a couple years ago. I read about it in the LA Times Book Review. The review was kind of snarky, I thought, yet it captured my interest. The story of a reclusive jazz pianist who had removed himself completely from society, with a plan for eventual suicide. That is, until a former lover left a baby, his baby, on his doorstep. It was romantic, dystopian, and funny. What inspired it?"

I didn't actually know what inspired that particular book. I just sat down at my typewriter and started writing, and it came out. Almost perfectly whole.

"Well, like I said, it resonated. It resonated because I know about that syndrome."

"What syndrome?" I asked Shirley.

"The syndrome whereby your child saves your life by virtue of just existing. Existing and providing love. We provide sustenance, yet the child provides the real sustenance, which is love."

"Oh Mom; maybe that is just hunger in a child's eyes."

"Don't be cynical, child."

"Perhaps," I said, "hunger is love."

"Perhaps. Perhaps it is thirst too," Shirley said, reaching into her bag and pulling out a flask. She undid the lid and poured some into her glass of lemonade. She reached out the flask toward me. I took it from her. I put it to my nose. It smelled like gasoline. Or something like gasoline. I tasted a little. I almost wretched and handed it back. She handed it to Dorothy, who took a generous pull.

"That's an interesting observation, Shirley. I never thought of it that way."

"You don't have children?"

"Mom. Give the man some air."

"What? What air? It just seems, from how he wrote about tending to an infant, that he had been through it before."

"Well, certainly not that I can recall," I said, sharing the inside joke with Dorothy. We shared a look too, which Shirley caught and then let go.

"Shirley. I have never raised a child. I can't imagine—or I can imagine, but that is all I can do: imagine what that's like. I think that raising a child must be the most rewarding experience possible. And you did a wonderful job, it seems. Dorothy is a grand young woman."

"I think so," Shirley said, and then took a sip from her hard lemonade. "I just followed her lead. She always indicated what she required. She's a great communicator, that one."

"Yes. I have noticed that." I still had the effervescence of her alcoholic drink lingering in my nostrils, which had me angling off-kilter. "She is very articulate, very precise."

"I don't know about that," Dorothy said, smiling. "My poetry teacher called my poems opaque."

Shirley said, "She got verbal very early, like at six months, or maybe a little later. She had invented her own language, and it had the same syntax and inflections of English. Yet they were her words. Her words alone. When I had to start sending her to preschool . . . well, she hated it. She cried and complained, still speaking in her language. In fact, she predominantly spoke in her language until she was four years old. One day I got to her preschool a little early, and I saw her speaking to another child. She was speaking her language, you know, but the other child was listening as if she understood Dorothy completely."

"Do you still remember your language?" I asked Dorothy.

"I remember speaking it, and I remember the process of how the words flowed naturally from my brain to my mouth and how it was exactly as if I were speaking English. Or French, which I also speak. Sometimes you can't find the right word, and so you wait until it comes to you. It was that way too. Then."

"When she started speaking English, she learned very fast and had a very large vocabulary, more of a vocabulary than most adults. Americans. But I missed her language so very much. I actually grieved for it." Shirley looked as if she were about to cry, but then began to laugh. "Such silly things we hold on to."

I picked up all the dishes to take them into the kitchen. Dorothy offered to help, but I told her that I had it. Besides, the way Shirley was drinking her hard lemonade, I had a feeling that she shouldn't be left alone. I don't know why I had that feeling. She wasn't acting particularly drunk, even though whatever she had in that flask of hers seemed pretty strong.

I brought in the dishes, washed them, and set them in the rack. When I turned to go back outside, Dorothy was standing there. She held in her hand the bottles of condiments: mustard and ketchup. "Well, she's done for," she said, as she pivoted and then put the bottles in the refrigerator. "Done for?" I asked. "Yep. Done for. She is really done for." She came and stood next to me. She stared curiously at my face. "Yep, can't deny the resemblance," she said. It was like she was looking in the mirror. I mean, when you look in the mirror and you study your own face, as if you were another person examining a face. It is a way of looking at yourself that no one talks about. I am sure we all do it. Not just those back from the dead. "What do you mean, she is done for?" I asked again. She shrugged and said, "She's out. She passed out."

CHAPTER 25

◆

Shirley had her head resting on her own folded arms. She looked quite peaceful that way. More peaceful than I would have wagered she was capable. "What are we going to do with her?" Dorothy asked. I thought I could take her to Minh's office and put her on the daybed there. But I didn't think Minh would have cared for that idea. I picked her up in my arms, the way a groom holds a bride, or a parent, a sleeping toddler, and carried her into the living room. She was very light. I couldn't imagine she weighed more than a hundred pounds. I laid her down on the sofa. She curled up.

"I'll go get her a blanket and pillows," I stated, staring blankly at her.

Dorothy touched my arm. "Thank you. You're a kind man. I don't think you could have killed anyone."

Upstairs in our bedroom; it consisted of a large king-size bed made from three-quarter-inch birch ply, unstained, and a night table made of the same: two pieces of wood and a top, and two shelves for books. The lamps I also made, from plumbing pipe and the guts of lamps found on the street. I went to a store in Queens that only sold lampshades and bought two lucent white dome-shaped shades, and in them fastened Edison bulbs. The dresser and the chifferobe I did not make. They were there when we moved in. From the forties. The dresser had a mirror that ran along on top. The dresser itself was made of maple, stained dark brown. It was long and had eight drawers. The mirror was tall and went halfway to the ceiling. I stood and looked at myself in the same way Dorothy had been looking at me downstairs in the kitchen. In the same way that I had seen Minh looking at herself in the same mirror. Bystander, objective, nominal. I must have looked at myself this way about a million times, in this life and my former life combined. It is part of the daily routine: combing hair, shaving, brushing teeth, and then standing back and looking. Looking and wondering: who is this? Is this me? Doesn't feel like it. I looked so different yesterday, and even only an hour ago when I caught myself walking by another mirror. I looked like a completely different person. Minh would purse her lips sometimes when she looked at herself. Sometimes she would catch me watching her and then give me a face, a scrunched-up face. She was radiant, always so radiant. And now she was gone. For how long? For as long as it took.

I heard a voice downstairs. On the staircase I could hear Dorothy's voice more clearly. But I couldn't hear what she was saying. I thought: it is rude to eavesdrop. On the other hand, I did need to know what it was they were after, if they were after anything. Minh thought so; she had said just as much. I moved closer, to just outside the room. I peeked my head into the room. Dorothy was sitting on the arm of the sofa. Shirley was sitting up. She was looking at Dorothy. Dorothy was speaking. Not quite in a whisper, but not full-throated. She spoke with a kind of matter-of-factness. The thing was, she wasn't speaking any language that I recognized. She wasn't speaking English. She wasn't speaking French. She wasn't speaking Greek or Latin or Spanish. It wasn't gibberish either. It had the same syncopation and syntax as English, and you could gather from her tone and inflection what it was that she was trying to convey. She was trying to convey to her mother a sense of calm, a sense that everything was going to be okay. For her mother not to worry. And maybe not to drink so much. All of this I gathered by interpretation and by translating the feeling that I got from listening to her.

"What about Minh?" Shirley asked.

It was quiet. Dorothy's back was to me, but I saw her shoulders go up and down.

The next morning, I came down to find that Shirley had made breakfast. Eggs, toast, bacon, and pancakes. And fresh-squeezed orange juice. Dorothy was at the breakfast table reading my Saturday *New York Times*. "Good morning," Shirley beamed when she saw me. She poured a cup of coffee from the Coffee Master and brought it over to me.

"Do you take cream?"

I nodded. "I can get it," I said.

Shirley went to the fridge and brought over the carton and poured a little juice in my mug. "There's sugar on the table," she said, as if this were her place. Her own restaurant or café or diner. Shirley's Joint, or something like that. I sat down across from Dorothy, who put down the paper—the real estate section—and said to me, "Good morning, Dad."

CHAPTER 26

◆

After breakfast, after my bike ride, I went up to my office to write. Dorothy and Shirley had gone off to the botanical garden in Prospect Park. I put some paper in my typewriter, a Remington Rand electric, which is even better than the IBM Selectric, the typewriter repair guy in Bay Ridge had told me adamantly. Michael, his name; Eastern Europe still hung to his tongue. I had brought my Olivetti electric to him for repairs. "Garbage! Not worth repairing," he spat. "The Olivetti Lettera 22 and 32 yes, but this no. Olivetti makes shit for electric." Michael insisted I buy the Remington Rand, and he cut off fifty bucks, selling it to me for one hundred fifty dollars. I brought it home like it was a newborn baby. Minh calls it the Mercedes-Benz of typewriters, and I can't disagree.

Sitting at my desk I thought: does Minh still love me? She is not here. Did she ever love me? Then I thought: when left alone with thoughts, one goes to darkness. Minh once explained this to me as the negativity bias. It goes back to earlier times in human history, when we needed to pay more attention to bad and dangerous threats in a world where paying more attention to danger was literally a matter of life and death. It is evolutionary, the tendency to dwell on the negative more than the positive. Just a way the brain has to keep us safe.

On the other hand, I am not a depressive or morbid, and my rational sense tells me that Minh does love me. This is based on the way she looks at me and the way she speaks to me, and even the way she left. That, too, was done out of love. Nevertheless, the thought lingered. Does she still love me? Or does she have another love, and that is who she went to?

And then my phone rang. It was Minh.

"Hello," I said. "Darling, where are you?"

"I am in Turkey at the moment."

"I have a question, and it might be a stupid one."

"Of course I still love you."

"Oh, that's good."

"I just can't be there now. You handle whatever this is."

"I am handling it."

"I know."

"When are you coming home?"

"When it has been handled."

"No matter how it is handled?"

"Yes."

"Okay. I love you, and please give my love to your folks."

I started back in on the novel. It was going in a strange direction, and the characters were in trouble, and I didn't know how to save them. I kept writing, describing their home, their car, their pets, their children, their neighborhood, where they went when they went out, their favorite restaurants and cafés and sports teams. And the way they made love, how they made love; I described this in graphic detail. The protagonists were a man and a woman, husband and wife. And there was a threat to them: an intruder. No, a space alien. No, a fascist takeover. I couldn't get to what it was, the crux of the matter. That was what the book was going to be called. At least I had a title: *The Crux of the Matter*.

I took the manuscript and threw it in the waste bin. Just a mess of words. It was nonsense. No real story. I took it out of the waste bin and put it in the bottom drawer of my desk. Dramatic gesture. Foolish. I put a fresh piece of paper in the typewriter. Chapter One, I wrote. I described a murder. The death of a painter. Stabbed in the heart. Found in his studio lying on top of a painting. The blood from his heart ran into the red paint on the canvas. This was better. A better beginning for a novel. It could go anywhere from there.

I wrote a good five pages, describing the motivations of the killer. Betrayal, envy, hatred. This painter had an affair with the wife of the protagonist and lured her away from him. Taking his child, the thing that he loved most in the world. His hatred of the killer was like an alien entity taking possession of the man. He knocked the painter down, like a linebacker crushing a quarterback, then took a large palette knife from the table where tubes of paint lay organized like Goethe's *Theory of Colours* and plunged it into the painter's heart. I sat back. Sat back and queried my subconscious. Was I describing what had actually occurred? It didn't seem authentic. So, I changed his death to be that he had fallen from a ladder, pushed.

That was what many readers wanted. Murder. Because it is the ultimate thing. Interesting. How one gets to that place. Removed from normal societal function. A biological short-circuiting. Instigated by extraordinary conditions. Choicelessness. Free will, either conscripted by evil or the other way around. The most godlike act possible, that of taking life away from another. And life is everything. As far as we know. It happens every day, many times over.

CHAPTER 27

◆

It was a cool evening, cool enough to get the fireplace going. Iridescent embers shimmering in the far end of the room where there was the hi-fi. I put on a record by jazz saxophonist Charles Lloyd and sat down on the sofa with a book. Lately my fireplace read was Anne Carson. *The Beauty of the Husband.* Was I so beautiful? I don't mean in the sort of snarky way Carson wrote about, but in a real way. Was I a good husband? I thought so. I mean, I was a good companion and true. I did the shopping and made the meals and even did the housekeeping. I didn't mind. What kind of husband was I before? When I was with Shirley. If I was this good, why would she have ever left me? I went through a period where my fireplace reads were Updike, Cheever, Bellow, and Roth: their narcissistic protagonists, all that adultery going on. Why was I reading those guys? They are fine writers and good storytellers, this can't be denied. But maybe that archetype—maybe I was one of those bastards. I didn't know. I guess asking Shirley was one way of finding out.

Dorothy came home. She set down her bag of books and sat beside me on the sofa.

"How was your day?" I asked nonchalantly.

"It was fine, I suppose," she said lackadaisical.

"Dorothy. Why did you call me 'Dad' in front of your mother? Does she know, or were you telling her?"

"She doesn't know, and I wasn't telling her."

"But what is she to think?"

"She is to think that her ex-husband, my father, is dead."

"She is to think that?"

"She does think that. She knows it. You are dead, the you who was you. He is dead because he died. Look it up."

"I don't need to look it up. I was there. Then why call me Dad?"

"It slipped."

"I don't believe that."

"Are you calling me a liar?"

"Not in so many words."

"In not so many words. And you call yourself a writer."

"Did anyone ever tell you that you are somewhat precocious?"

"That's what I mean. Somewhat? Get real."

"I happen to like the word 'somewhat.'"

"Why? What for? How?"

"It's a placeholder."

"I suppose."

"And you like the phrase 'I suppose,' I have noticed."

"I suppose."

"We need placeholder words. To gather our thoughts, but also in order to not reveal any more than we want to."

"I guess you are a writer, then."

"And what about you? What are you? How do you see yourself?"

"I only see myself when I am looking in the mirror. And barely, at that."

"I know what you mean."

"I'm sure you do."

"So, Dorothy, what's the agenda? What are your plans? Are you looking for something?"

"I have already found it. And you are starting to sound like Minh. Where is she, anyway?"

"She went to visit family."

"To Vietnam, to Hanoi?"

I nodded.

"For how long?"

I shrugged.

"Because of me?"

"Not quite."

"Because of my mom showing up."

"She is unsure of your motivations and of the potential consequences of this exposure. If what you are saying is true, then I was wanted for murder."

"Not exactly. You were a suspect, but then you died."

"So when you die . . ."

"You are no longer a suspect. Or the case against you is closed. Look at Lee Harvey Oswald. He was the lead suspect, then he died, and the case was closed."

"But were there other suspects?"

"Yes."

"Your mom?"

"Yes."

"And . . ."

"And they dropped it. They dropped it when Antonio's family took his body back to Argentina."

"What do you think?" I said, standing to stir the logs in the fireplace.

"I don't know. Just like I am not convinced that Lee Harvey Oswald killed JFK. I mean, he could have. That was a pretty easy shot in spite of what Oliver Stone says. Have you ever been to Dallas? If you follow that route, the route Kennedy's motorcade took, you see that he was a sitting duck from a sixth-floor corner window. Sitting duck. But they killed Oswald, and there never was a trial. So we will never know. I know that people said they thought they heard a shot from the grassy knoll, but sound ricochets. I'm just saying we will never know. At this point we will never know. The Church committee came to the conclusion that chances are there was a conspiracy. Well, no shit. Do I think you killed him? I mean, look at you. Not this you. Can *this you* be that much different from the old you? The you who died? That's the million-dollar question."

I walked back over to the sofa and looked down at her and said, "You didn't answer my question."

"Can you just believe I came here to meet my father? Is

that so hard to believe? I know Minh is worried, and I don't blame her. She loves you. Anyone can see that. So she wants you to sort through it. Which is what you are doing. Everything will be okay. I would never ever ever want anything bad to happen to you."

"Yes, but what about Shirley?"

"I can't speak for her. And I can see why you might be concerned. She is not stable. She has never been stable. I have seen her do some really bad things. Well, not really bad. But. Bad. Not nice. But you just let me handle her. Do you want me to send her back home?"

"Yes. No. Not yet. I need to know a few things."

"Okay. That's what I figured. But be careful. Be very careful."

I told myself that I had nothing to fear. That anything that might, or could, happen had nothing to do with me or my fate. It just was. It already was. Augustine: memory is going backward, from future to past. That's easy to say but more difficult to fully comprehend. Still, in many ways it was a comfort, that idea.

CHAPTER 28

◆

I had never been so happy in my life. At least, as far as I could remember. Minh snuggled close to me as we lay postcoital in the over-large king bed. I had treated myself to such expansiveness with my first advance on royalties, after sleeping on a single for some twenty years. I was ready for it. Yet, we were at the very edge of the bed. And the thing that I feared, the idea of sleeping next to someone and having them in my space, to literally have a fraction of the space that I was used to occupying—it didn't bother me. In fact, I was as happy as I could ever remember being.

It was early morning on New Year's Day. We had gone to the opera, *Rigoletto*, and then had dinner, and then the New Year's Eve countdown celebration back at Café Luxembourg. And then back to my place in Windsor Terrace. We made love for the first time. Afterwards we lay clenched like spring vines. I put my hand on her behind, ran it along the smooth curvature of it, feeling the firm, soft smoothness of it. Reaching down between her legs where it was wet. She was ready, and somehow, I was ready, again. Yet that is not what made me as happy as I could ever remember being. It was holding her close and seeing her sleeping face, and knowing that I had never seen anything more beautiful.

So I held that memory close and wanted to get back to it, repeat it in the Aristotelian sense: memory is a state of affection conditioned by the lapse of time. Or, in the Nietzschean theory of eternal recurrence, we will live through all of the worst and best memories over and over again. What does that say about my past? Is it worth it to relive the worst along with the best? I say so.

I was missing Minh. Her touch, her looks—she had so many different looks. More than anyone I had ever known. The external conditions of light and time of day and situation, and her mood and my mood, and what she was wearing and how she was holding herself in conjunction with whatever, wherever she was in mind and mood, in space and energy. Sometimes, at the right angle, she was a child, and of course this made me feel different things. Being older than her, I did sometimes take on a paternal role, or rather, I assumed it. And of course this was completely disengaged from any kind of romantic feeling. When she felt aroused and wanted intimacy—this was another look. And always, or almost always, I would wait for her to make the first move, to initiate sex, making love. It had to come from her. I could perhaps help that process along by cooking a good meal or by buying her something nice or writing her a lovely poem, or . . . I couldn't know. She might tell me later. And then I might be on the sofa reading a book, and she would take the book from my hands and set it down, and then she would straddle me. Sometimes I might be doing dishes and she would come up from behind and put her arms around me. When I was alone, I had a fantasy of someone coming up from behind me while I was in the kitchen cooking or doing the dishes and putting their arms around me, squeezing, and whispering in my ear, "I love you." And then it happened.

But then again, how do you really know anyone? How can you possibly know what motivates, inspires, directs, and guides them?

I knew Minh. We had been about as intimate as two people possibly could. I had told her everything about myself, all of the secrets, all of the mundane. She had told me quite a lot about herself as well. What she thought about when she was alone, those private, sensual thoughts. She told me about her relationship with her mother and how it had been fraught at times. Now she had come to realize that when she was younger, she took a narrower view, concentrating on the negative. She worked through that negativity bias and came to realize what a warm and loving mother she had. This was a woman who survived the most violent, darkest days of the Vietnam War. And from the wreckage she became a successful businesswoman and one of the most widely published poets in her country. True, her mother was against the idea of Minh marrying me. I might have been against it, for that matter, if I were in her shoes. Yet when she saw that Minh had made up her mind, she supported her fully. After all, Minh had been on her own in this country since she was fourteen years old: boarding school, Ivy League, and now Columbia. So she knew her own mind and was perhaps wise beyond her years. But then again . . . I don't know exactly. I can't know, except to know that she picked me.

She picked me. I wouldn't have dared approach her. That night when she broke the ice at Café Luxembourg I went right with it. And then with everything after that. The multiple times she broke things off, I quietly acquiesced. She would, after perhaps days and sometimes only hours, want me back. And I would be only so willing. After all, it was either her or complete aloneness. I was okay with either but much preferred her to aloneness.

That is why, when she brought up the idea of marriage, even with a few initial doubts I readily went with it. I could imagine it, a life together. Even though I had funds, my bank account wasn't bountiful. I had spent the greater part of my advance on the things I had never had, or don't remember ever having: a car, travel, clothes, books, stereo system, and a nice apartment in Windsor Terrace with a yard and a dog. We were married, but she kept her place in Park Slope at first. Better for her to study for her last year in the MFA program at Columbia. And when my novel did well and was licensed to Hulu for a series, and her novels took off we bought our house in Ditmas Park.

I died, and then I was reborn. I came to NYC, walked into a job in a book and record store and got a first-rate education—self-education—in matters of literature, art, music, and history. And I wrote as if there were something guiding my hand.

CHAPTER 29

◆

It was a good day of writing. Yet harrowing. The psyche of this killer, this husband, this betrayed dunce, this abrogated father, this closet nihilist; if it was me; was it me? It was now, now that I was inhabiting his modus operandi. Guiding him through the day. Long days alone: morose, scoring drugs, succumbing to the stupor, to the wasting of a soul, the trashing of an intellect, rationalizing mayhem and murder. He smells it, the blood, the vengeance, and what is better than killing the painter—the painter is really just collateral damage, mostly innocent—but killing the real perpetrator, the malicious spouse, that doesn't add up; it doesn't set things back right. Nothing could, except killing her dream and fantasy, that was as close as he could come to true retribution.

Thinking about the character analysis of the killer actually made me sick to my stomach. I was forcing myself to do it, but it went against every shred of my will. I felt like Sisyphus. I had cheated death and this was my punishment. To inhabit the mind and body of a killer. At least on the page. Well, that was it. I wasn't going to do it any longer. At least not for the rest of the day.

I went downstairs and there was Shirley at the base of the stairs, standing next to the dog, Humphrey. They stood waiting, both with heads tilted. Shirley reached down and patted Humphrey's head and said, "Hello, Geronimo. I just got back and the door was open, so I came in. I hope you don't mind." I walked past her and into the living room. I put on a record by Van Morrison, *Moondance*. "Of course I don't mind, Shirley.

After all, you are staying here for . . . how long are you staying?" She came into the room and sat down on the sofa. Humphrey jumped into her lap. "I am leaving next week," she said. I gulped. "Did I say next week? I meant tomorrow."

I sat down on the chair across from her. "I love this record," she said, as her head bounced to the jazzy rhythm of "Moondance."

"I love it too," I said. "In fact, this next song, this song, 'Crazy Love,' I sang it to Minh at our wedding."

"Crazy love, now that's something I know something about." Humphrey jumped down from Shirley's lap and bounced into mine.

"Isn't all love a little crazy?" I replied to her statement.

"I think I'll have a cigarette. Do you mind if I smoke on your porch?" she said, pulling out a pack of American Spirits. The desire for a cigarette struck me, even though I could not remember ever having smoked one.

She sat in Minh's chair on the porch. "Do you mind if I have one of those things?" I asked her.

"I didn't, or wouldn't, think that you smoked." She pulled one from the pack and handed it to me.

"I don't. Or I haven't. I just have an urge for one."

"You probably miss Minh and are stressed."

I took the cigarette from her. She handed me a pack of matches. Written on the matchbook were the words "Fort Defiance." I lit my cigarette and handed the matchbook back to her. It did not taste, in the least, like what I thought it would taste like. Not as harsh. It smoldered like the dying ashes in an urn. Tasted awful. Yet, I liked the way the smoke felt trapped in my mouth. I liked the way, as a cloud, the smoke mushroomed from my mouth and surrounded me before dissipating.

"Yes. I miss Minh. She will be back."

"When?"

"I'm not sure. She is with her family in Hanoi."

"Oh."

"When you said you know about crazy love, what did you mean? If you don't mind my asking."

She made a motion with her hand holding the cigarette. "Do you have an ashtray? I'm done with this."

"No. Not really. But I'll get something. Care for water or a seltzer?"

"A seltzer?"

"Yeah. We have one of those SodaStreams—make our own. I drink a lot of seltzer," I said proudly.

"That's nice. I'll take a seltzer."

I went into the house and into the kitchen. I poured two glasses of seltzer and grabbed an empty jar for the cigarette butts. I handed her the jar and she put her cigarette in it. I took the cigarette from between my lips, where it had been this whole time, and dropped it in the jar. Handing her a glass of seltzer, I poured some of mine into the jar, dousing the cigarettes. "You were saying?"

"What was I saying? Oh yes. Crazy love. Yes, it is true, I know that. I had some bad luck. Well, not luck. Well, I guess you could call it luck. Is there such a thing as luck? Or is it just fate? Either way, at a certain point, I made my bed. But I didn't sleep in it. I always found another bed to sleep in. I was married, you know. When I was quite young, younger than Minh and not too much older than Dorothy, I met this man. A published poet, not widely published, but he was a poet. He wrote for a small newspaper. I met him at a bar in Long Beach, California. He seemed too handsome to be true. Tall, long neatly trimmed beard, and red hair, like you, though his hair had more of a sheen to it. He was sure of himself, but quiet. I had to instigate the conversation, you know. Yet there was something that attracted me to him. Even though he was not like anyone I had ever been attracted to before. I had always gone for a more macho kind of guy. Well, guess what? I ended up marrying the poor guy."

"What happened?"

"We had a kid. A daughter, Dorothy, named after his grandma. But. Well, I had this art gallery in Santa Monica. I started spending more time there. He quit his job and just took care of Dorothy full time. But then I fell in love, or I thought I fell in love, with this artist from Argentina. A painter from Argentina. He was my archetype, or what I thought my archetype was: tall, dark, and handsome with really big muscles with tattoos of naked women and Jesus all over his bronze body. And he was rich, rich and successful. I left my husband and took the kid. Probably the worst thing that I ever did in my life. Because, though I didn't realize it at the time, it was he who I truly loved, but by the time I came to realize this, it was too late. Both men were dead."

"Well, hey there," I said to Dorothy as she walked up to the porch.

"Well, hello," she answered back. "What are you guys doing?"

Shirley lifted up her glass. "Just drinking seltzer and spinning yarn."

"Oh," I said, "I didn't realize that was a yarn."

"Yarn, reality, I don't know the difference anymore."

"Oh, Mom," Dorothy said. "You're so full of shit. Where can a girl get a seltzer?"

CHAPTER 30

◆

I received word from my agent that Hulu had picked up the option for a second season of my first novel. On top of that I thought I had made a breakthrough with the new novel. I spoke with Minh. She congratulated me. There was a tinge of sadness in her voice though, which I asked her about. But she said not to worry. It was just that she missed me, Humphrey, and home. She said, "Babe, don't forget, I love you." I needed to hear that. It helped to quell the tide of melancholy that I knew was coming my way with more days away from her, for, I didn't know how long. I didn't know because I didn't know how to be rid of Shirley. It was like the Henry Miller novel *Devil in Paradise.* The only thing was, and I was beginning to realize this, I was stuck with her. We had a daughter together, and whether she knew this or not we were inexorably linked. So it was best to revel in these small successes in my professional life and not think too much about the other stuff. At least not until I came up with a solution. Otherwise I would be inconsolable. So, I ordered Indian food to be delivered.

We sat around the dining table with the saag paneer, kachori, chicken tikka masala, and navratan korma in round plastic containers, the garlic naan in foil. After I had set these things down, Dorothy started laughing inexplicably. "What's so funny, daughter?" Shirley asked.

"I just thought of something, and it made me laugh."

I opened the containers and sat down. I started things off by dumping some rice on my plate.

"The comedy of life is subconscious. Men figure they know why they exist. Laughter is the wisdom of sublime reason." I put some saag paneer on my plate, to the side of the rice, and said, "Picabia again?" Dorothy nodded.

"You are fucking obsessed with Picabia," Shirley said.

"I am. And what of it?"

"Are you a Dadaist?" I asked, though I knew that she was not. Her personality profile provided much more clarity, more specificity than the Dadaists. She shared an irreverent sense of humor, a cynicism. Ultimately I felt that she was too romantic to be a Dadaist.

Knowing that I knew the answer to my own question, she changed the subject. "So, what were you guys talking about?"

"When?" asked Shirley, who then put a forkful of chicken tikka masala in her mouth.

"When you were on the porch. Were you telling Geronimo your life story?"

"Not all of it, my dear."

"That's good."

"Don't be cheeky."

"I love when she gets like this. It's like we enter a Noël Coward play," Dorothy said. "Cheeky."

"You know about Noël Coward? You're so young and—," I said before being interrupted.

"I know a lot of things that people wouldn't assume I did."

"Yes, well, maybe. Sometimes it is best to have some circumspection. You know what they say."

"No, Mother. What do they say?"

"About children being seen and not heard." This made her laugh. And her laughing made Dorothy laugh, and Dorothy's laughing caused me to laugh too.

"As you said, or Picabia said, 'Laughter is the wisdom of sublime reason.'"

We noshed for a little while, not talking, just making funny faces at each other. Words seemed like a contrivance at this point. At least that was how I felt, and I got the feeling that they both felt the same way.

"Mother, Mother!"

"What is it, my child?"

"You have to see it. You simply have to see it."

"What?"

"Them!"

"Just let me finish my tikka masala, please."

Dorothy watched her as she put a forkful into her mouth ever so delicately. She set the fork down.

"There, there they are."

"Well, isn't that lovely. And so many."

"Have you seen them before?"

"Of course. But it has been a while. And never like that. It's like a wall of flickering light."

"Enjoy it now," I interjected. "Probably they will be gone soon enough. End of summer and all."

"Summer ends much later these days," Dorothy said sadly.

"That's because we fucked it up for you."

"Mother, you didn't fuck it up."

"I meant the preceding generations, the generations preceding you."

Shirley went inside the house. I stood there with Dorothy looking at the fireflies. Dorothy sidled up to me. She put her arm through my arm. "I think I am in love," she said.

"Oh."

"This person at school. They've bowled me over."

"That's nice. In love eh?"

"Well, you know. Smitten. When did you know that you were in love with Minh?"

"It sounds funny and maybe a tad pretentious, yet I think I have always been in love with Minh. It just never occurred to me that someone like her could exist. In moments of solitude, or lonely moments, before I met her, I would try to conceive of what it would be like to be with someone, and what that person might be like. And it is Minh, only more so. I didn't know what I was doing was manifesting my dream."

"How did you do that?"

"I can tell you exactly how: by not caring. By completely letting go. By accepting that I might always be alone, and to be okay with that. That quality attracted Minh to me because she is that way too."

"That sounds very romantic," Shirley said, joining us, clutching her flask. "But the cynic in me thinks it's bullshit. Then again, what do I know?"

"Did you love my father?" Dorothy asked.

"What a question! What a question. Let me think. It was so long ago . . . Yes. I suppose I did. How could you not love that man? I loved him so much that I hated him. Or hated it. Or hated myself."

She took a pull from the flask and handed it to me. I took another whiff of it. Ghastly, I thought. I handed it back to her and then she handed it to Dorothy, who declined. "I guess I'm drinking alone. Again."

CHAPTER 31

◆

"Have you guys ever been to Coney Island?" I asked, wanting to get out of the house and wanting to separate Shirley from her flask. I told Shirley that she would have to leave the flask behind because I couldn't drive with an open container. Couldn't and wouldn't. I told them to wait in front of the house and I pulled the Benz from out of the carport, backing it out of the long driveway. I had recently done some body work on it, plus new tires and new springs in front. And more importantly I put in a Tesla powertrain, converting the car to electric. Backing into the street, I pulled up along the curb to where Shirley and Dorothy stood. Shirley got into the front passenger seat and Dorothy into the back.

"This is a very nice car. Things have gone well for you," Shirley said with no trace of bitterness. Truly impressed.

"Yes, things have gone well for me. But I have had this car since before all of that happened. It may not look it – this car is over thirty years old. It's a '97 and has close to three hundred thousand miles on it. Many people will tell you that the late nineties S320 is the best of all Benzes. Back when all the parts were still made in Germany."

"Does it bother you to own a car by a manufacturer who also manufactured tanks for the Nazis?"

"I guess we all have things in our past that we are not so proud of," Dorothy said pointedly.

"Yes. But the Holocaust."

"Whenever I come across morality, I seek out instinct."

"Can we please do without Picabia for a few hours?"

We drove along Ocean Parkway. There wasn't much traffic on the street on a Sunday night at around nine o'clock. I put on a Curtis Mayfield cassette. The Benz still had the original Becker sound system. This cassette was Minh's favorite. I had made it for her. It made me sad to play it, but also made me feel close to her. "Oh, oh, oh, oh!" Dorothy gasped. "Can we pick up Towson? It wants to go to Coney too."

Shirley turned around from the front seat to face Dorothy. "It?"

"Yes. It. Towson is an Animist. In other words she believes that everything has a soul. A rock, a chair, a spoon; and we refer to all of these things as its. Why are humans any better than say a tree? One could argue quite the opposite. Therefore she is an it."

"Are you an it?" Shirley asked incredulously.

"Yes. But I am also a woman."

"A young woman," I added.

Shirley asked, "And from where do you know this Towson?"

"Towson is this person in my philosophy class and it lives in Kensington. I messaged it that we were going to Coney Island. It's on the way. Is that okay, Da . . . Geronimo?"

I pulled off of Ocean Parkway and headed back to Kensington. We pulled up in front of Dorothy's friend's building. A big apartment building. Big and nice, with manicured grass and a little plaza in front of it. Towson ran up to my car and got into the back seat. Towson had a very friendly demeanor. "This is a very cool car," Towson said. "Thank you," I replied. "My father had one of these. Mom made him sell it. It was even older. I think it was from the seventies. There was nothing wrong with it, but she said it wasn't practical, and he didn't want to convert it to electric. Plus we couldn't take it on long drives. Dad said it would be alright, but Mom didn't trust it. Not after it broke down one time when we went to visit Grandmother in Baltimore."

I liked Towson already. How many people knew about these cars and appreciated their aesthetic? Dorothy and Towson began talking in hushed tones. I couldn't make out what they were saying and turned up Curtis to give them some privacy.

Coney Island was all lit up like a movie of Coney Island, and at the center of it all was the Wonder Wheel. I parked in a secret parking lot behind Nathan's Hot Dogs. It cost fifty bucks cash, yet it was worth it. Minh and I went on a regular basis. We liked to go watch the Cyclones play. The Cyclones, the Mets' Single-A team. Young players on their way up and old ones on their way out, taking one last chance to work their way back to the big game. The crowd was relaxed and as loose as the quality of play. Minh and I would each bring a book and watch disinterestedly. The air was sweet by the ocean, even on the hottest summer day. This day was hot, a hot September evening. The ocean breeze made it wondrous.

We walked along the boardwalk looking at all the people. The people, none of them pretty, seemed straight out of a Fellini film. Shirley pulled her flask from her purse. She gave me a guilty look before she took a big slug. All the while Towson and Dorothy seemed to be entranced by the lights and the people and each other. Shirley said, "I really need this. I kept it in my bag on the ride over. Don't be mad."

I looked at her and felt like admonishing her. But who was I? "I'm not mad, Shirley. I just hate to see you do that to yourself. I think that you're a better person than you give yourself credit for. I mean, just look at Dorothy. That's a great person, and you raised her."

She laughed and said, "But she called you Dad."

Towson and Dorothy came running up to us and said in unison, "Let's go on the rides!" I looked at Shirley. She shook her head back and forth, eyes closed. "Okay. I'm game."

I told them that I would beg off. I had been on one of those rides, the one that shoots you up in the air, spins you around, and shoots right back down with g-force. I did this as Minh watched from below. She told me that it was traumatic for her to witness. I told her she had no idea. But I took out my credit card and bought the three of them wristbands.

"You have to at least ride the Cyclone with us," Dorothy said pleadingly.

"We'll see," I said.

"Spoken like a true father," Towson said teasingly.

"Yes, but . . ." Shirley motioned to me with her thumb, "He's not her father." And then let out a big guffaw.

I walked to the water. The sounds of boom boxes blasting grooves echoed off the buildings along the boardwalk. Sounds of people laughing, screaming, shouting. Sounds of bells and whistles of unknown origin all made for a strange calliope of discordant music. The moon loomed large above the water. In it I could see Minh. It seemed like everything was reminding me of her; the moon in particular. Once we had taken a house on Shelter Island, and on the deck on a clear night, with that same moon overhead, she told me that it was a blank piece of paper or a luminescent orb. And you could see anything that your heart desired in it, when it was big and full like that.

My phone rang, or chimed, the tone like a cascading arpeggio. It was Minh.

"Good morning," I said.

"Good evening," she replied.

"Is it yesterday's morning or tomorrow's evening?"

There was quiet on the line.

"Are you okay?" she inquired, and though I felt okay, fine, I obviously was not.

"I'm okay. As okay as can be expected."

"Where are you? Sounds interesting there."

"Coney."

"With your family?"

"Don't call them that."

"Sorry. Just teasing."

"You're my family. My only family. The only family that

matters to me."

"That's not accurate or true. What's important is what matters now. I am your family. I am your wife. We are a unit. Nothing will change that."

"Unit. I don't think I have ever heard you use that word before. At least, not in relation to us. You chastised me when I called us a partnership. I want you to come home. I don't like this."

"I'm sorry about the 'unit' usage. But she is your daughter, thus making her your family."

"Okay. I will give you that, I suppose. But I need her mother out of here and out of my life."

"That is your ex-wife."

"You mean my widow."

"Okay, both. That just means that she will never be out of your life. Not entirely."

"That sucks."

"Tell me about it. But, it will be alright."

She told me that she would be home soon. After we hung up, I sat down in the sand and crossed my legs; I put my face in my hands and cried. I couldn't remember the last time I cried. I heard my name cried, being shouted. "Geronimo!" like they say in war movies when someone is jumping from a plane. "Geronimo!" I stood and turned to face the boardwalk.

There I saw Dorothy cupping her hands and shouting "Geronimo! Mom went crazy!"

I ran up to her, "What happened?"

"We were on this ride. The Coney Clipper, they call it. It goes back and forth, you know. We had already been on a couple rides which were far more radical. But for some reason, this one triggered her. And as it swayed fast through the air, she just started screaming her head off. Not a fun scream like other people were doing, but a bloodcurdling scream, like you know in the movie *The Fly* where she sees her husband's head and it is a fly's head. Like that, only worse. And she was screaming and telling them to stop the 'fucking boat.' It was so loud and so terrible. So they did. And she climbed out of the thing, not waiting for the person who worked there to unbuckle her. She ran up to him, knocked him down, and then started pummeling his face with her flask."

"Oh, dear lord."

"And then she threw up in his face."

"Where is she now?"

"In police custody. There is like a holding place they have for unruly customers. Towson is with her."

"Has she been arrested?"

"No, not formally."

"How can that be?"

"Because after I pulled her off the guy, she came to her senses. She realized what she had done. She reached into her handbag and pulled out a bundle of hundred-dollar bills. She gave me ten of them and told me to give them to the guy, asking him not to press charges. I did, and he agreed."

"So, what are the police doing with her?"

"Giving her a citation for an open container."

"Oh."

CHAPTER 32

◆

On the ride back things were quiet in the car.

"I search for silence in the midst of noise, playing deaf until I am deaf myself."

Shirley, Towson, and I said in unison, "Picabia."

Shirley took a stick of gum from her purse and put it in her mouth and started chewing the piece dramatically. "I suppose I should apologize."

Nobody said anything.

"Could you put Curtis back on?" Towson asked. I turned on the Becker.

The Curtis song "Keep On Keeping On" came on. We drove along the Belt Parkway listening to the music. In the rearview mirror I saw that Dorothy had fallen asleep on Towson's shoulder. Towson looked out the window. Shirley, too, was gazing absently out her window. Maybe they were listening to the music – probably just trying to digest what had just happened. Towson had witnessed shockingly cruel and in fact insane behavior by Dorothy's mom, and yet leapt into the lurch by being there for both Dorothy and Shirley. By sitting with Shirley while she was detained. Something a family member would do. And never, as of yet, made any judgments on Shirley's behavior.

"My brother is bipolar," Towson said as if it was reading my thoughts.

"Oh yeah?"

"They have him on lithium, which he hates, but he takes it."

"How old is he?"

"He is fifteen. He is very sweet most of the time, but he had a few incidents that were traumatizing, for all."

"You guys know that I am sitting here. And I am not bipolar. I am just volatile and perhaps an alcoholic. But that's my business."

"It's not your business," Dorothy said with eyes closed and her head still on Towson's shoulder, "When we have to intervene with the authorities."

"I took care of things."

I dropped Towson off. It was midnight. Hard to believe that everything that had happened at Coney Island transpired in less than three hours. When we got home, Dorothy went off to bed without a word.

"Do you want some tea?" I asked Shirley. She nodded, and I put the kettle on the stove. My beautiful Viking stove. The kettle had a mirrored surface; whenever I caught a glimpse of myself on that shiny surface it made me chuckle. How did I get here? I'd ask myself. I took great pride in this kettle and washed it after every meal cooked on the stovetop in case that some oil or other kind of grease might blunt its sheen. I wanted to always have that reflective surface unmarred.

I filled the kettle up through the filtration system connected to the sink's water pipes. I checked to see if Shirley was watching. She was not, and I looked at myself in the kettle. Yes. There I was. The me who was experiencing some kind of reckoning. Or was about to.

I put the teapot on the dining room table, where Shirley sat absently staring through the sliding door at the backyard. A lone bird was making a hooting sound. "What is that?" she asked? "An owl?"

"No, that's a dove," I told her.

I poured her some tea from the vintage teapot which had what they call an atomic design on the side. Why atomic? Because, I suppose, of the universal obsession with things atomic at that time—the atomic bomb and thus the threat of nuclear annihilation that inspired art and design—or at least, the appropriation of the word as a way of describing things from that era. Wittgenstein tells us that an atomic face is a combination of entities and things, atoms of meaning that correspond to the basic elements of reality. Personally, I just liked the aesthetic.

"So, what triggered your episode?" I asked Shirley nonchalantly as I poured the tea.

"What kind?"

"What kind?"

"What kind of tea?"

"Oh yes. Chamomile."

"I get it. Calming. The idea that I need calming."

"I just like it before bed."

"Was that something that Minh introduced to you? The idea of tea before bed?"

"Yes, now that you mention it."

"Where is this Minh?"

"She is away visiting family."

"That's nice," Shirley said without any inflection. She took a sip of the tea and then blew on it to cool it, and then took another sip. "You asked me something? I forgot."

"What triggered you? Back at Coney Island, Luna Park."

"These rides, these rides. They are terrible and a kind of torture. It wasn't that man's fault, but I took it out on him. It had been welling up. Each ride was a little more violent than the one preceding it. But this last one, the swaying back and forth. It shook me. I needed it to stop, and it wouldn't stop, and so I lashed out. It was wrong of me, and I do feel bad about it and that poor fellow. Hopefully, that thousand will do him some good."

"I think you need some help."

"Yes, in the old days, you could just go to a sanatorium in the Alps for a few months. Like Zelda Fitzgerald. Now there are rehabs for the rich, but that is depressing. Those places are way stations in between binges."

"Are you rich?"

"Oh yes. Very."

"What happened to Dorothy's father?" I figured I would

just ask. I wanted to hear what she had to say, and I was tired.

"Dorothy's father? Dorothy's father. I was very cruel to him. After having Dorothy, I went back to work in the gallery immediately. So, for that first year it was just Dorothy and her dad every day. I would come home for dinner after a day in the gallery, and on weekends. But more and more often, I wouldn't come home for dinner. I think I really began to resent their bond and was even jealous of it. Even though I was the one who sort of created it."

"What was his name?"

"His name was Gerald. He was medium build and medium good-looking and just . . . medium. But he had an Achilles' heel."

"What was that?

"I can't really say exactly; there was something that made me want to hurt him. That's what I mean."

"That was *his* Achilles' heel?"

"I mean that I fell for Antonio, and I took my child and left him. And when he contested in court, I made up charges that he molested Dorothy. Complete fiction. But I had a lot of money and he had none, and so my lawyer crushed him."

"You mean *you* crushed him."

"Yes. I mean I crushed him. And he didn't recover. He was left with nothing."

"What happened to him?"

"He died. Heroin overdose."

"Does Dorothy remember him?"

"She says she does. But she was so young, I don't see how she could."

"And Antonio? What do you think happened?"

"I really can't say."

"Can't? Or won't?"

"Jesus, Geronimo. Can't you tell I would really rather not talk about it?"

"Actually, I think you do want to talk about it. You need to. Maybe that is why you are so unsettled."

"Yeah. Well, what about you? Your whole story is pretty far-fetched. Right down to your name, Geronimo Vang."

I wasn't looking for trouble, and I didn't want to open a can of worms, and so I chose to end the conversation. "It's been a long day. We should probably just go to bed."

"Yes. Good idea. I probably won't see you in the morning. I am going back. Early flight. I just want to thank you for everything." Then she looked at me as if seeing through me and started speaking as if to someone else.

"He died. He fell off a ladder in his studio. It wasn't such a shock. I mean, it was unexpected, but he drank a lot. And he made these large and tall paintings. Paintings of mountains and skies and skyscrapers and women—not Cubism, but akin. When I say tall, I mean like thirty feet tall. I had to rent a new studio space just to accommodate them, an old foundry building in San Pedro. I found him after he had been lying there for a few days. Not too pleasant."

"You sound so removed when talking about it."

"I am. I was removed. It was like a painting in a painting. He had fallen off the ladder and simultaneously tipped a can of red paint, which washed over him on the gray concrete floor. It looked like a bloody mess, but in fact there was no blood. Just blunt trauma to the head. The police suspected foul play at first. That's what they do. And my ex-husband was implicated. He had been seen near the building the night of. And he had no reason to be around there. But then he died, and the family took Antonio's body back to Argentina. They said to me, '*Que los muertos entierren a sus muertos.*' Let the dead bury their dead."

"What did they mean by that?"

"He was an atheist, so in many ways they already considered him dead. They were all too happy to have him buried. They didn't think too much of me either."

"Life is strange."

"Is it? Seems like everything happens like it is supposed to. Anyway, I'm tired. And I don't really feel like talking about the past and all of that malarkey."

CHAPTER 33

◆

The next morning Shirley was gone. The air in the house felt purified, like a ghost had come in the night and swept it clean of murkiness. I made coffee in the Coffee Master. Frothed some milk in the frother. Dorothy came into the dining room, holding her suitcase and her tote bag, which said "New Yorker" on the side.

"Good morning, Dad," she said while setting down her things.

"Good morning, Daughter." I poured her a cup of coffee and ladled some froth on top.

"I'm going to miss your coffee."

I refreshed my cup with coffee. We both sat down at the counter side by side.

"Why are you going to miss it?"

"Because I am moving out. I'm going to move in with Towson. Its roommate just left, which is a charming break of luck."

"In Kensington?"

"No, that's where its parents live. In the East Village."

"Oh, okay. Well, that seems good. Much easier commute."

For some inexplicable, or maybe explicable, reason, tears began to well up in my eye sockets. I had only just made her acquaintance, but she was my daughter, and now she was leaving before I had really gotten a chance to know her.

"Dad, don't cry. I'm just moving out. I'm not leaving you again. You are not going back in time to when you had no daughter."

"Feels like it. But if you say so."

"I say so." And she leaned over and kissed my cheek.

I mumbled, "Our heads are round so our thoughts can change direction."

"Dad, you've been reading Picabia."

"Yes. Thank you for introducing me to Francis."

"Of course. I love Francis. And I love you. Dad, don't forget that. See, your past came back, not to haunt you – to bring good news. Are you glad?"

"Yes. Very glad. And I want to stop pretending to be someone other than what I am. Or who I am."

"Don't you see that who you are now is actually more authentic than who you were then. You have chosen this person. You had a say, as an adult, in how you were to be. You inspire me."

"Our heads are round so our thoughts can change direction."

"You said that."

I wiped my nose with my shirt sleeve and said, "Why did you say that Antonio was stabbed in the heart?"

"Sounds more poetic than falling or being pushed off a ladder."

"You're an interesting person. And a bit mischievous."

"You think?" She gulped down her coffee and said, "I better go to class."

"I'll walk you to the subway. Me and Humphrey."

We walked through the tree-lined streets of Ditmas Park. Dorothy was already swinging her arms like a real New Yorker when she walked; broad strokes back and forth. I offered to carry her suitcase, but she demurred. The sun glinted off her red hair like infrared light. I felt somehow tremulous and also exuberant, as if walking wholly into another dimension.

PART THREE

CHAPTER 34

◆

The house was empty. It felt as empty as anything I had ever known. Emptier than my consciousness immediately after I died, or thereabouts. Even the dog, Humphrey, seemed barely there. I called his name; he wouldn't come. Asleep in his dog bed, or just staring blankly out the window in the living room. Or not blankly, expectantly. I felt abandoned. Where had my inner fortitude gone, that self-generating sense of well-being? That whole mechanism had been dismantled, and I was a little pissed about that. I started to make a plan as to how to get it back. I had to go back, in my mind, in my memory, to when I had it. And there was one day that marked the time when it was at its peak, when that inner fortitude was strongest. That was the night I met Minh.

That was also the night I began to understand happiness, true and meaningful happiness. It didn't happen that night, but the wheels were in motion. I just didn't know it. And then, nine months later, as if gestating a baby, we were married. And that, too, was sheer happiness, every moment. There were moments of anxiety concerning work and some expenses, yet never a moment of not being happy in my life with Minh. In fact, that happiness, contentedness, ameliorated any anxiety; cleared the rising tenseness in my chest, which is where the anxiety manifested, and would dissipate.

But now, unhappiness and even a little anger. Yes, but only just a little. She had left me. She asked me to leave, leave my past, and when I didn't, she did. Only she didn't. She told me the whole time that she was coming back, and not contingent on them leaving. Just coming back. And now they had left, and she wasn't here. And I was alone. All alone with myself. Like in that Lenny Bruce bit: all alone. You dig? I'm really going to swing and get some of that shiny black furniture, a bullfight poster, and get a coffee table and make a door out of it. A stained smoking jacket and a pearly white phone, and I'll sit back and relax, and finally I'll be all alone. And that's the best way to make it: all alone, all alone. Oh, what a joy to be all alone! I'm happy alone, don't you see? Yeah, right.

My cell phone chimed Minh's chime.

"Hello."

"Oh, hello."

"What are you doing?"

"Just swinging, baby. Just swinging."

"Oh, that's nice. Are you on drugs?"

"Oh, no. Just watched a Lenny Bruce video on YouTube."

"All alone. Nice. So, they left?"

"Who? Oh, them. Yes."

"Do you miss me?"

I laughed.

"What's so funny?"

"Baby, I am going crazy without you. I miss you so much, my eyes are bloodshot, and I haven't even been crying."

"Well, if you missed me so much, why aren't you at the airport?"

"At the airport?"

"Yes. To pick me up."

"You're at the airport?"

"Didn't you get my email?"

"I haven't. I didn't. I have not opened my computer in, well, I don't know how long. You're at the airport?!"

It was late afternoon. The cool, crisp autumn air felt good on my face, smelled good in my nose. I rolled the windows down, the double-paned bulletproof windows. This car was the favorite of diplomats and gangsters for that reason. I put on a Rolling Stones cassette; "Get Off of My Cloud" came on. Yeah, that's right! Forces from the past, get off of my cloud, motherfuckers! I pulled up to the Turkish Airlines arrival lane. There was Minh, wearing her Christian Dior sunglasses, sitting on one of her red vintage Samsonite suitcases. She got into the car. She took off her sunglasses and leaned over, presenting her cheek to me. I kissed it, and then she turned her head to face me, and I kissed her flush on the lips. It was a long kiss, time-wise. It was passionate, almost like a first real kiss. And in some ways, it felt like one.

We got home. Humphrey went into convulsions of joy. Jumping up on Minh, making tiny spirited circles. I put down her luggage and took her in my arms.

"Miss me?" she asked again.

"You don't even know."

We sat down on the sofa. "Tell me about it," she said.

I told her what had happened, all of it. She laughed like I was telling a joke with an elongated punchline. After I had finished, she asked if I felt some relief. Only some, I told her. I told her that I was thinking that maybe I wanted to make a clean reckoning of things, of coming clean, of making a public statement and letting the chips fall where they would. If I were to be investigated, so be it. If I was found culpable of a crime, so be it. Did the public deserve to know my story? Minh asked, and then answered her own question; of course they did not. It is not so uncommon for a writer to protect their identity. Look at Elena Ferrante.

I saw her logic, as always. And so I decided: from that day forward, I wouldn't try to run or hide from any other revelations. I would also just live my life every day the way I wanted it to be lived. The way Minh and I wanted it to be lived. On the other hand, what happens in the night, or at the end, when you are alone again—who's to say that this coupledom, this twosome, this blissful union will always be? Of course it won't; just hard to fathom that, at that moment. In the moment which is temporal, that is fleeting. In it, when in it, time is irrelevant, or not pertinent. The only thing that is pertinent is the feeling, the sense of well-being – of being with someone with whom you feel comfortable. So much so that it is like being alone, the same comfort. And when making love, when Minh and I make love, it is something else, heightened. When I am inside her, when we are one, it is intense. And then the dog, Humphrey, jumps on the bed and barks at us, thinking we are playing, and wants in on it. We laugh and I kick him off the bed, and then just like that we are back in it. Back in the passion, back losing ourselves in the passion. The place where time stops. No one else can understand that, except those that know it, or have known it.

Things happened in the world during this time that might have thrown everything off, might have thrown us off-kilter. Though I got wobbly at times, I maintained equilibrium. Miraculously.

I was working on the Remington Rand. Things were moving briskly now. Early on, I said to myself: just get one page done, one page done a day. And I did most days, with a few unexpected interruptions. And then Minh got back, and things returned to some normalcy. I had to start again with writing just one page. Prior to the visitors, I was cranking out three, four, five, and even six pages in the morning and maybe another page or two in the evening. The momentum was strong, and I was cranking out pages on the Remington. The characters were based on actual humans, their names barely changed. They were telling me what to write, they were telling me what they were doing and telegraphing to me what they were going to do, what they were about to do, or what they might do, if provoked. The protagonist and his wife were so happy all of the time they were together, and happy apart knowing they would be together. They stopped distrusting their happiness, and this made them even more happy. I stopped distrusting that a novel about a couple who was so happy might be of interest, could be interesting, could be entertaining. And no matter what we say to ourselves about great literature or even pulp fiction, the common denominator is that we go to be entertained. And entertainment is pleasure, is pleasurable. In T. S. Eliot's essay on the social function of poetry, he says that the function of poetry is that it has to give pleasure. If you ask what kind of pleasure, the answer is the kind of pleasure that poetry gives.

And all the while my protagonists were so happy, Minh and I were as happy and as content as we had ever been, and I was cranking away on the Remington Rand, and then it stopped. Stopped completely. An electric typewriter is not like a regular typewriter: without power, it does not work, not at all. I lifted the lid, touched the letter ball, and moved the scroll. I didn't know what to do with it or how to coax it back into working for me. I had been so lost in the work that, coming out of it, I thought perhaps my fervor somehow caused the thing to overheat or something. That was a dumb idea. I picked up my phone to call my typewriter repairman, Michael, the old Russian guy who lived out in Bay Ridge. I had bought this typewriter from him, and he was the one who always got it back up and running.

Just as I was about to dial, Minh came into the room. "Power is out. Did your typewriter blow a fuse?"

"Impossible."

"Yeah. You want to check the fuse box?"

"Yeah, sure."

I got up from my desk, the desk I had made from a sheet of three-quarter birch ply and plumbing pipes for legs. I came around the desk and took Minh in my arms. She nibbled on my ear. I got aroused; that was my sweet spot, and she knew it. I lifted her skirt. "No panties," she whispered in my ear. I pushed aside some of the things on my desk, almost knocking the Remington Rand to the floor. I lifted Minh, put her on the desk, she wrapped her legs around my hips, and we fucked.

We did it in my chair and then eventually wound up on the Persian rug. We fell asleep there in each other's arms. I had a dream that I was an air-conditioning repairman. It was the fifties, and Minh answered the door in a floral-print summer dress. Same house as ours, or almost the same. She showed me the AC unit in the living room; indeed, it was on the fritz. The fan worked, but no cold air was forthcoming. I turned to tell her the bad news, and she was completely naked. We ended up on the floor, which was covered in books. She got on top of me and kissed my chest all over. Then she straddled me and put my member in her. It felt so good that I screamed in pleasure, making her laugh. But then something jagged jabbed into my butt. I reached back around and pulled out a hardcover of Thomas Wolfe's *Of Time and the River*. "First edition," Minh said, and took the book from my hands and threw it across the room.

We woke up and the room was dark. I got up and attempted to turn on the desk lamp in order to find my glasses and my copy of *Of Time and the River*. The light did not turn on. "Power is still out," Minh said.

CHAPTER 35

◆

We put on clothes, got Humphrey, leashed him and went outside. He looked perplexed, as if he knew something was awry. We walked down the block. It was around 7 p.m., not dark but also not light out. All the homes, it appeared, had no power. Many people were out on their porch; these houses in Ditmas Park mostly all had porches, and some of the fortunate ones had wraparound porches. Though Minh and I had lived on that block for almost three years, we didn't know the people who lived there. There wasn't any of that waving from the porch, "Hey, neighbor!" Yet people were friendly enough. One man wearing a suit and tie who looked to be just home from work, holding his bike, rolling into his driveway, greeted by his partner or husband, saw us walking and said, "Blackout." We looked at him, wondering if he was talking to us. "The whole city is out. I just rode from Wall Street. Everything is shut down."

We walked to the bodega. The man who was always there, a nice fellow from the Middle East, who I had barely said a passing word to in three years, who at that certain time of day, knelt in front of the store for prayers. So you had to time it. He was inside and greeted us very warmly. "Take ice cream! Take as much ice cream as you can carry! It won't last."

"Really?" I asked.

"Yes. But of course."

"I'm scared," Minh said to me as she put her arm through mine as we walked on Argyle Street, back to our house. It had gotten much darker since we began our outing. We could hear the voices of the people on the porches, some of whom were illuminated by candlelight.

"There's nothing to be afraid of. Everything in the dark is there in the light."

"Thanks, Dad," she said, sounding a little snarky, unusually so.

"Okay."

"It's more than simply darkness or a blackout. The blackout represents something else, something that has happened or is going to happen. I do not have a good feeling in the pit of my stomach."

"Well, let's see. I don't discount this feeling or sense of yours in the least bit. In fact, since you brought it up, it made me get past the fact that we have all of this free ice cream. And in the pit of my own stomach, I feel that, yes, something is perhaps not right. I mean, usually blackouts come in the summer, when the grid is overloaded by everyone having air conditioners blasting. Obviously, that is not the case."

"Yes, and since the riots by right-wing extremists at the end of summer, you know, there have been all kinds of threats to the infrastructure. How the Russians are now in league with the Not Fucking Around Coalition. Their whole operation has gotten more sophisticated."

We got home. I put the ice cream in the freezer, hoping it would at least keep it cool enough for us to eat before it got too runny.

"There's no internet, no reception of any kind. Can't even make a phone call. I'm a little frightened," Minh said, holding her iPhone 20.

I didn't remember ever hearing Minh say that she was scared. Not even during Hurricane Donald when our elm tree was lifted straight out of the ground and carried a half a block before being set down on a Toyota Camry. Nor when there was the second siege of the Capitol, when the president had been abducted and there was a state of lockdown. The uprising was put down because of the double agents who had infiltrated the Not Fucking Around Coalition, the Oath Keepers, and

Proud Boys; not the U.S. military or the FBI or the CIA but mostly men and women of color and white women from the South who had organized their group in secrecy for years, sacrificing friends and family to achieve complete authenticity in that undercover movement. The Christian nationalist groups accepted people of color as long as they were ardent enough in their hatred of anything that smacked of wokeness. The second uprising was put down and the president rescued; she finished her second term without any other domestic disturbances. Minh never was alarmed or scared. I was scared enough for the both of us.

Minh didn't say she was scared when the Spectra virus came and ripped through America. Probably because it affected mostly white men. The management of everything had to be revised. Through every branch of the government. And even the upper echelons of corporate businesses. The white male patriarchy was effectively replaced. And though I too got ill, somehow I did not get too sick. My Mexican blood helped to save me. That and the healthy diet we lived by. But I did get sick. Minh tended to me with wheatgrass and oregano tablets, and I was fine after a week. The majority of white males, though, were not. Five percent died, and another ten percent were rendered disabled. The rest of the white male population had an existential crisis that left them unable to continue with life as they had known it. It was compared to the polio epidemic. And again, Minh never got scared.

The cause was eventually determined: a taint in the cattle industry, bacteria of unknown origin that spread ubiquitously, and then the bacteria reacted to yeast in beer that somehow triggered the virus. Since I didn't drink beer, Minh wasn't sure that I was affected by the virus at all. She thought that I just had a bad cold. Either way, it decimated the white male population and caused the ones who weren't affected to grow reclusive and apathetic. Women and people of color filled the vacuum. Since then, the machinery of government has been running much more efficiently and with a kind of equanimity that this country had never seen before. And when taxes were raised to pay for social programs, health, and education, very few complained, since white men had almost literally lost their voice, and all reaped the benefits of a more stable and even contented population. I know Minh and I were happy to give a large chunk of our income for a better society.

And then Hurricane Donald tore through the East Coast causing terrible destruction and loss of life. We had gone to a friend's house in the Catskills, thinking we would escape the power of the hurricane, which was projected to hit NYC and the beach areas of Long Island. But the storm knocked out the power lines up north, too, and in the darkness with the howling of the wind and a sky that seemed to be screaming, I was very frightened. But Minh stayed calm and comforted me. She did not scare that easily, that woman.

Because of the terrible damage caused by Donald and the other storms and droughts and hurricanes and fires, President Harris and the government began to pour billions of dollars into the climate crisis and the new Department of Planetary Solutions. With the advent of a device that sucked carbon out of the atmosphere, and the aviation and auto industries finding green alternatives almost overnight, the coal plants permanently closed and replaced with solar grids with nary a song of protest from the whites, the climate crisis and its repercussions miraculously began to subside. And since then, the whole ecosystem has stabilized.

But now, with this power outage, Minh sensed that something was not right. The cell phones were out. How could that be? Fortunately, because of a book called *The Little Book of Hygge: Danish Secrets to Happy Living*, which called for candles and a hearth and plenty of firewood for the fireplace, and to have pastries and lots of chocolates on hand, we were all set. We nestled by burning cedar logs in the fireplace, noshing on a bar of dark chocolate, sea salt, and almonds, and losing ourselves and our worries in gentle necking.

As we cuddled, Minh began to laugh. "What's so funny?" I asked. She had so many different variations of laughter. There was the chuckle, which sounded almost like a strong case of the hiccups. There was the giggle, which was a cartoonish he-he-he. There was the long vowel that led into a triumphant ha-ha-ha. And sometimes there was the cycle, which began with the giggle and then morphed into a chuckle, and finally the long vowel, which resulted in a belly laugh, which is what this was. My question to her seemed to cause a kind of convulsive laughter which was infectious. My laughter did not express itself outwardly; it was almost silent, without any kind of accompanying noise. And yet, my body shook.

She quieted. "I don't know why I started cracking up so," she said, regaining composure. "I just thought of President Harris's speech, you know, after Hurricane Anderson. After all the destruction, she said, 'It's time to cut the shit.' Just flat out, and then announced the formation of the Department of Planetary Solutions. And how she said that so plainly to the American public. Just thinking of it made me laugh."

"Well, there have been results. Tangible results. And I am sort of stunned. And so happy about it. It seems that since we have been together, not only has my life become as wonderful as I could have ever hoped, but the conditions of the world have improved markedly."

"Such a crazy coincidence. I often think about that. But now, for some reason, I feel a certain foreboding."

CHAPTER 36

◆

Sitting in front of the fire, recounting all of what we had been through and the extraordinary turn of events not only to me, to her, to us, but to the world at large—I couldn't help but think that I had done something wonderful to deserve all of it. I thought of our first meeting at Café Luxembourg, and how it was she who broke the ice by asking if I was a writer, and all the subsequent hours we spent together. On New Year's Eve, that first New Year's Eve together at the Metropolitan Opera watching *Rigoletto*, she with her hair pulled back, looking a bit older than her years. Me in my dark suit and pomade holding my red curls in place, how I was beaming to be with her, looking younger than my years. Though I didn't quite know how many years there were between us, I knew I had more than she. And she woke up in my bed on New Year's Day. They say that how you spend New Year's Day is how you will spend the rest of the year. Or the rest of your life.

In those early days and nights of the new year, spending many of them together, getting to know one another yet already feeling that there was an intuitive knowledge of each other's core. Aware of the fantasy that occurs with young lovers, or young love: that of romanticizing the partner, making them into something that is idealized. And then, when that facade crumbles with revelation after revelation, one could be disappointed. Yet that facade never crumbled. In fact, it gained luster and still does.

The days passed. No electricity. We lived off of seltzer water, coffee, chocolate, fruits, and vegetables that were readily available at the grocer's. Word of mouth spread: something had happened with the solar grids as a result of some flaws in the wires used to make the transition from the former power grid to the new one. The government had assigned spokespeople to street corners to hand out mimeographs and to make announcements. Basically, telling everyone to hold on, and that power would be restored soon. The hospitals still ran on stored generator power, and there was no shortage of food, since veggies, fruit, and canned goods were made available to all. Nobody panicked, at least not in our neck of the woods. In fact, things were quite cozy.

I got out my old Olivetti Lettera 32 to work on. And my novel-writing resumed. Minh, who liked to work shorthand, mostly for brainstorming purposes, had no trouble making the transition from laptop to notebooks to continue her work. And we made love throughout the day. It was like a strange kind of honeymoon.

As the days passed, Minh's fears also subsided. It seemed to make sense that there would be a hiccup when making such a huge transition of power. The things that propelled our lives, what we had come to rely on to make our lives more comfortable, also distracted us from the really beautiful moments happening all the time.

I told Minh that I was writing about us, barely disguised. "Is it a romance novel?" she asked. I had never thought of it as such, yet it was. I was writing a romance novel, and that was the one kind of book I hadn't read, except for the writers from the Romantic period: writers such as Laurence Sterne, Samuel Richardson, Maria Edgeworth.

"You might like Sally Rooney or Louise Masters or Beth Sargent," Minh told me.

"I did enjoy Sally's *Normal People*. I guess I am closer to, say, Henry Brooke's *The Fool of Quality*."

"I'm not saying that you should read more contemporary literature."

"No, I think I should. Do you have any suggestions?"

"I'll make you a list," she told me.

One morning, Dorothy and Towson showed up. I found them in the living room, sitting by the fireplace expectantly. They were bundled in heavy coats and both wearing wool caps, which they later told me they had bought from a street vendor for five dollars. They looked most bedraggled.

"Hello Dorothy. Hello Towson."

"Hello, Father," Dorothy said in a sedately playful manner.

"Hello, Mr. Vang," Towson said.

"It was freezing in our place."

"I'll get a fire going." I pulled out the kindling and newspaper from the pine box I had made to store those items, and then three pieces of wood from the cord of wood. On a metal hook that hung above the fire, I placed a kettle of water. "Coffee? Tea?" I asked them.

In unison: "Coffee."

"How long do you think this will last?" Towson asked me.

"I'm not sure. How long has it been?"

"Eight days," said Minh as she entered the room. "Would you like some scones?" Minh offered.

"Oh yes, please," said Towson.

"Dorothy?"

"I am starving. Literally."

"Literally?" I inquired.

"No, not literally. We have been eating the not-so-frozen food from the not-so-frozen freezer. You know college kids—we live off that stuff."

After everyone had some coffee and the scones that Minh had made, we went out to the front porch. Humphrey sat in Minh's lap, gazing at Dorothy. "Well, go ahead," Minh told Humphrey, and the dog jumped down from her lap and leapt into Dorothy's. Dorothy started petting Humphrey and started to weep. Little convulsive breaths and big fat tears. "Don't worry," Minh said. "Everything is going to be alright."

After a proper breakfast, we all went back out to the front porch, each one of us with a book. Towson sat on the swing reading Gwendolyn Brooks's *Annie Allen*. Dorothy sat on the steps reading Paul Schrader's *Transcendental Style in Film*. Minh sat on her rattan chair reading Renata Adler's *Speedboat*, and I was not reading *Monday or Tuesday* by Virginia Woolf. I was not reading because I was sneaking peeks at this group. The women, each consumed with an earnest desire to tell a story, their story, by some kind of transference to page. Literal, analogous, epigrammatic, or by capturing images that represented the action from present to past to future.

Towson was a poet. Its mother was a poet, and its father was a documentary filmmaker, which is what Dorothy aspired to and what she was studying at NYU. Towson's father recently produced for PBS the *Frontline* segment on the virus that had decimated the white male population in the U.S. He had won a Peabody for that. But its parents had to move to DC because its mother had gotten a teaching position at Georgetown, and the father was working on a film about the new Department of Planetary Solutions. Through Towson's parents' connections, Towson had landed a position as Poet Advisor to Maggie Drake in their successful campaign for president. In this capacity, at a campaign event, Towson would read a poem before Drake spoke. Maggie Drake became the first non-normative person elected to higher office. The highest office.

"I want my poetry to be alive. It is like shared consciousness. When people hear my words they are becoming me. They embody through hearing and also sight our shared essence, the thoughts, ideas, words, sounds, vibrations, harmonics, all that goes into making the visceral quality of poetry. That's what I want to do with my poetry."

"That's *what you are doing* with your poetry," Dorothy said reverently.

During breakfast, Dorothy announced that she wanted to begin a documentary about Minh and me à la *Grey Gardens*. "Is that how you see us?" Minh asked incredulously, though not without humor. "Two aging eccentric recluses?"

Dorothy explained, "Well, I do see similarities. Please don't be offended. Sometimes it seems that one of you could finish the other's sentences."

I laughed. "I assure you, I never know how Minh is going to

finish a sentence."

As this conversation progressed, I became more uncomfortable. Not for myself, but how I felt Minh would react to such a proposal. Even though I knew that young people, and, in fact, all artists of all ages, might say that they have an idea for a project, it is quite rare that there is follow-through. I sensed that Dorothy was inspired by her idea, by her classes at school, and by Minh and me. Also, by telling our story, she could tell her own story, and that was the point, wasn't it?

"Well," Minh began, "Do you want to know what I think?"

"Yes. Of course."

"I think that it is a very good idea, and I am okay with it if Geronimo is. Though I think that it would be best to leave out his history before he died."

Then both of them looked at me expectantly. Expecting that I would be in agreement with Minh. "I say yes, sure, you go ahead and make your film. Like the Maysles did, cinema verité, fly-on-the-wall, you know, and then whatever comes out comes out. Direct cinema. And shoot it for, say, six months so that you can have plenty of footage. When you have opportunities to shoot us. Then what you put together will be true and honest. I think that it might be quite boring for most, yet I want to support you. It is—it's nice to have a subject. A willing subject."

"And you are both willing?" Dorothy asked, looking at Minh.

Minh nodded and said, "Let's hope that the power comes back on, because you will need to charge your batteries."

Dorothy went to her bag and pulled out a 16mm camera and started cranking the stainless steel lever on the side of it.

"Is that a Bolex?" I asked.

"Yes. Super 16."

"So we are starting right away are we?" Minh interjected.

Dorothy smiled and said, "Why not?"

I suddenly felt self-conscious. Who would ever see this student film? Potentially many people, considering the subject—Minh and me—as we were both well-known enough in the public media slipstream. Still, I had my reservations. "Okay, but don't forget. Only for six months."

"Geronimo," Minh said, looking at me intently. "Why don't we make it nine months?"

"Nine months?"

"Yes."

"Nine months. Oh! Nine months." I went over to her and held her. I kissed her eyes, then both cheeks, and then her lips. We looked at each other. She smiled and nodded. I then noticed the sound of a machine in the room. I looked up and there was Dorothy, with her Bolex, filming us.

CHAPTER 37

◆

A day later, the power came back on; Dorothy and Towson returned to their apartment in the East Village. There seemed to be some sort of cosmic shift. Now that people had been ten days without cell phones or computers, it was like their psychic sense had been washed. It wasn't just the way that I was feeling, it was also in the perceptions of my neighbors, whom Minh and I had gotten to know in these last ten days. Marty and Henry, who lived a few doors down, concurred with this observation. Henry was a watercolor painter who made greeting cards; he said he had gone back to oils and couldn't stop painting. Marty, the fellow who worked on Wall Street, who we had seen on the first day of the blackout, said he was considering quitting his job. There were the Strouds: Frank and Elizabeth, and their three children, Aloysius, Hudson, and Tristopher. They had a big dog named Ben Thorpe, who our dog, Humphrey, loved to romp with. And the Roses: Beth and Sue Ellen, and their twins, Fresh and Duty; and the Denesens: Irene and Major Ford - all of them would be out every evening. Now when we strolled down Argyle Street, we not only got plenty of hellos, but also a few stop-and-chats, which both Minh and I quite enjoyed. A lot had changed since the blackout, not just an almost-complete transition to solar power.

Minh had agreed to go to Los Angeles to meet the people who were producing a series based on her last book, *The Continuing Adventures of Mai, The Superhero Supergirl, Part 5*. Rather than be alone again, I asked to go with her. "Of course, my love!" she said as she put a hand on both of my cheeks, pulled me forward, and kissed my lips.

We took one of the new solar jets. Whereas a trip to the West Coast from NYC used to take somewhere between five and six hours, it now took closer to eight because the solar power provided less thrust with a smoother ride. And because of that, the airplanes were designed for greater legroom. There was no more first class; everyone rode first class. The airlines had a new policy, because there were fewer flights, that to qualify for a ticket, you had to have racked up points using the high-speed rail or not have flown in the last year. Since Minh and I hadn't flown in a few years, we were good to go. The airlines also made exceptions for other circumstances like big life events, but because the new solar planes took longer to reach a destination, you might as well go by high-speed rail. The thing that was interesting with the solar planes was that, theoretically, they could stay up in the air for weeks, months, even years.

Since there had been such a mass vacancy for pilots due to the Spectra virus, the airlines had a new program to train flight attendants to fill the pilots' roles. To fulfill the need for flight attendants, there was a new program for kids who got an early diploma from high school to go to work on the planes and take part in the new college self-education program. After working on the flights, the young people could stay at hostels set up through the airlines and host countries, where they could learn languages and study art and culture in various countries. Also, young people already in college could opt for this program as well. All of these new innovations in education and technology were having not only a big and positive impact on the climate— they were having a big impression on the morale of young people and on the population in general.

We flew into Burbank Airport, where you got off the plane on the tarmac and then walked inside the building to retrieve luggage. We walked out onto the tarmac. It was a warm November day. The air was fragrant; it smelled like eucalyptus trees. It was my first visit to Los Angeles since I had died. I thought that it might trigger a Proustian rush of memories.

I felt nothing in that way. Minh looked at me as if she were reading my thoughts. "You feel nothing." I nodded.

Minh had a few meetings with her West Coast representatives who handled the work which had been optioned for streaming. I also had my first meetings in person with the folks at the production company. It was all very exciting. Los Angeles seemed like another country. So different from New York City. Sprawling, clean, tidy. The beach at Santa Monica was nothing like Coney Island. Everyone dressed in stylish bathing suits, talking to one another calmly, the music from loudspeakers played ambient sounds, the vendors on the boardwalk sold green drinks and smoothies.

We had a rental car, one of the new solar-run Matrix vehicles. It was a different animal than my '97 Benz. Still, I preferred my Benz, mostly for sentimental and aesthetic reasons. With the Matrix one didn't even have to drive. You just entered the destination and the car took you there. There was a steering wheel covered in plush velvet, which was mostly just something to hold onto. In California there were only certain stretches of road and highway that one could operate a vehicle manually. "Let's drive to the desert. Let's drive to Joshua Tree," Minh said.

The car took us through Palm Springs. We were both amazed at how immaculately the previous centuries' middle period architecture had been preserved. "These buildings are cool," Minh said. "Anything striking a bell of reminiscence?" I shook my head. I felt something. A sense of glee, and I thought that perhaps it was just experiencing something truly wondrous. But nothing Proustian, or déjà vu-ish. As we got to the edge of town, a tone sounded and a light came on saying that it was okay to switch to manual driving mode. I put my hands on the steering wheel and put the car into gear.

We drove through Yucca Valley and into Joshua Tree National Park. "It all seems familiar," Minh said.

"That's because they filmed a lot of sci-fi films here. I guess these odd cacti and giant slabs of rock are what filmmakers presumed things on Mars might look like."

"Actually, from pictures I have seen, not so far off, save for the Joshua trees. What about you, Geronimo? Does any of it seem familiar?"

"No, nothing. Not at all. I feel nothing, except gratitude. Gratitude at being here with you and knowing that my life before was troubled. Now, in your presence, and living the life we have, well, I know I could face any ghosts or demons, but they are just not here. At least I don't see or feel them."

CHAPTER 38

◆

"How was LA?" Dorothy asked at dinner on our first night back.

"It was groovy," I said unseriously.

"I liked it," Minh said. "Shiny and clean, like what I imagine Atlantis might have looked like."

"Do you miss it?" I asked Dorothy.

"Oh god no. I hated it there. Couldn't wait to leave."

I took a sip of an Arnold Palmer and asked, "How's Towson?"

"Ze ze is great."

"Z?"

"Yes. Ze. Ze is what Towson is using instead of it now. Ze as in zero, zero preconceptions, as in Generation Z, as in Zoom, as in . . ."

"As in Zany," I said dryly.

"As in Zesty," Minh interjected.

After finishing the pizza from Di Fara and the salad that I had thrown together from the garden, I stood to gather the plates. "So, when do you start on your project?"

"What?"

"Your film project, us?"

She started laughing. "I have already started. Didn't you see the Sony XS-900 on the tripod?"

I looked around and in the corner of the dining room was a camera on a tripod. "Oh yes."

"That camera is awesome. It shoots wide, and with new editing software I can make it look as if the camera were handheld, getting close-ups of you and Minh and even cutaways of the interior of the room, or of Humphrey on the ground cleaning himself. I can make it look like *Grey Gardens!*"

I cleared my throat. "Maybe in the future you can give us a heads-up."

"Or," Minh said, "we can just assume that we are always being filmed."

"And you're okay with that?" I asked Minh.

"I don't see why I wouldn't be. Life is art and art is life."

"So art for art's sake?"

"No. I don't believe that. I believe in experience for art's sake. All of this is experience. We are living it. And if she films it then she is experiencing it; as will be anyone who views her work, her final cut."

"Okay," I said. "You know, sometimes I think I know your fears and trepidations and want to be protective. It just goes to show I don't know, not always. Okay then. Let it roll."

"I only ask that you be present when the camera is rolling. I don't want it to feel like we are under surveillance," Minh added.

"Agreed," Dorothy said emphatically. "Besides, mostly I will be holding the camera. I just want to try different approaches. I have a lot of high-tech equipment at my disposal through NYU."

We went about living our lives. On the weekends and during the week, on most days after school, Dorothy would be there with her camera. There is something about being filmed that brings out the Edith Beale in you. Even if you are normally restrained, or even introverted, suddenly you become preternaturally expressive. Making proclamations to the other persons such as:

Me: "What shall we have for lunch today?"

Minh: "I don't know, why don't you make your delicious guacamole."

"And quesadillas with queso from the Mexican store."

"Yes, after all it's in your blood, *mi vida.*"

And so on and so forth. Until Dorothy implored us to act naturally and forget she was filming.

Things got more real after the first month. Minh started feeling not so good. As her pregnancy developed the physical reality of having a creature growing inside her began to take hold and the reality that a thing, a person, was infringing on her psychic autonomy kind of bummed her out. The thing that was her refuge, her sacred space, was now compromised; at all times. Even when she meditated, it was there. When she slept, more poorly with each passing day; when she ate, this craving for peanut butter sandwiches, Fuji apples, and limeade, guava nectar, dolmas, and popcorn with yeast on top, and pho for dinner every night. I didn't mind, and did everything I could to make sure that her every desire was fulfilled, even going so far as to learn how to make pho. No easy task to do it right. Minh walked me through it as she made the first few batches. But since she was sleeping more and more it fell on me to make it. It took a while to get it just right. My first attempts were not acceptable, and after Minh rejected them I had to go to the Vietnamese restaurant a few blocks away and do a complete study. Eventually I became, if not a master pho chef, at least proficient enough.

And she slept a lot. One thing that I always admired about Minh is her ability to nap. She was like a cat in that way. She could nap pretty much anywhere. I have seen her, in a crowded noisy bar, put her head on her folded arms and grab a micro-nap. In the morning after reading the paper and drinking half a pot of coffee she might grab forty winks. And Humphrey is only too happy to join her in these kips. They cuddle up and off they go. She told me once that, "You Americans don't know about the nap, always running around; in Vietnam the whole country has a doze after lunch." I didn't know if this was true, but it sounded reasonable. I have always felt guilty about napping during the day. That is, until I met Minh. And now I have come to believe that napping, and frequent napping, is the key to mental and spiritual health. If, after a good night's sleep, during the following day you grab a couple catnaps, your whole nervous system is in a constant state of reawakening to the wonderments of life. With her body being taxed as it was,

she took napping as far as it could go and spent the majority
of the waking day napping. Yet her naps were not always so
relaxing as her body got more and more morphed. And this
made her a little irritable, which made her very apologetic. I told
her not to worry. Not to feel bad if she snapped at me, which
she did on occasion. But never nastily or derogatively. And she
was not snapping at me, just toward me; she was snapping at
God, or whatever contrived this process of mutating her body to
grow another.

Dorothy caught a great deal of this on camera. She also
caught us talking about our hopes for the child and about
our plans on how to raise it, and how we seemed to be almost
completely in agreement on these issues. Except for one
point. Minh thought that when the child was older it should
go to boarding school. "Unless he or she is not bright," she
said laughingly. The idea did not sit well with me, yet since
we were so many steps away from that decision it caused me
little concern.

CHAPTER 39

◆

We never knew exactly when Dorothy was coming; it seemed like when she wasn't there we were rehearsing for being back on camera. Even in the bedroom, where make-believe and different kinds of scenarios had always been part of the play. That didn't change, except we now pretended to be on camera when we made love. What if we were? What if Dorothy had put one of those sneaky devices on the wall or in the mirror or who knows where and how. It was already strange making love when there was another person-to-be in Minh's body. Whatever was going on with her, her hormones and physiology made Minh even hornier than ever, which is saying a lot. All of it, the pregnancy, the documentary, the successes of our work, the new presidential administration, the first elected Ze president, the new solar energy infrastructure, the post-blackout reduction of electronic activity among the masses. More and more people, it seemed, were participating in the new trend of staring into space. Whereas before people would stare blankly into their phone, now they stood or sat in public spaces and just stared into space. Not for long, for a minute or two, and then off they went. Staring into space, like napping, helped one recharge their batteries.

All of these developments filled me with excitement. What excited me the most, aside from Minh's pregnancy, was my novel, of which I had just completed the third and, I thought, final draft. In the novel I combined the story of the happy married couple with the murder story. All of it taken almost explicitly from my own life. Barely adorned. So close was it to my story that I knew upon publication it would be a big story, and in interviews or in press around the release I would come forward with the truth, or what I knew to be the truth, of my story.

We were in the living room, looking at art books and listening to a Bill Evans record. Dorothy got her camera out. She walked over to the record player and lifted the needle. "Sorry, copyright issue with the music." She picked up the Canon and started shooting. She came close to where Minh and I were sitting on the sofa.

I asked Minh if she wanted to read the manuscript of my new novel.

"No thanks. I just can't concentrate these days. I wouldn't be doing you a service."

"That's okay. But listen. I'm coming clean."

"Coming clean?"

"Yes. I'm telling the whole story, as far as what I know. Even about the murder of the painter."

"Does that put you in jeopardy?"

"No, not really. It was ruled an accident."

"And yet."

"And yet I feel that it wasn't."

"And you want to find out the truth about it."

"I have to."

"And by putting it in the book it will open up the case, and you think that perhaps it will get resolved?"

"I think that one of three things happened to the painter. Either he was drunk and fell off the ladder onto the concrete floor and cracked his head, or Shirley pushed him off the ladder, or I did. The I that was me then."

"How do you find out? How does anyone find out?"

"I don't know."

"Did you write about Shirley in the book?"

"Yes. There is a Shirley character."

"And?"

"And she is not going to like it."

"What do you think she is going to do?"

"I think she will try to come at me. In some way."

"She still loves you."

"She still loves Gerald, who is not me. But she will think it is still me."

"And you're picking this time to do this?"

"The book won't come out until after the baby comes."

"Okay. I mean, I believe you know what you're doing and I trust you."

She put her face in her hands and started to cry. I put my arms around her and held her for a minute. I said, "I can scuttle the whole thing too. If you'd rather."

"It's not that. I'm just scared."

"Scared of what, darling?"

"Scared of it: childbirth."

"I know. They do have new drugs, so that you won't feel a thing yet will be totally conscious during birth. And a new epidural that makes the birth passage almost elastic, so that nothing, you know, tears."

"And you'll be there in the hospital?"

"Oh darling, of course, you know I will be."

"I know."

CHAPTER 40

◆

We were watching the final round of the international staring contest between Lithuania and Vietnam. To the applause of a packed auditorium, the two players entered from either side of the stage and sat down on two Wegner Wishbone chairs facing each other. The Vietnamese player was a young woman with a decidedly playful face whose name was Thanh Nuyguyen. The player for the Lithuanians was an older man with a full head of hair and a brown graying beard. His name was Matis Jurgis. The two players dressed in the uniforms celebrating the national colors of their countries. The player for Vietnam wore a red and gold jersey with number 9 printed in black on her left breast. Lithuania wore a yellow, green, and red Polo with the number 11 printed in white in the center of his chest.

Matis was heavily favored, having set the record for longest stare without a blink. One hour, eleven minutes, and fifty-three seconds. Thanh's longest stare was fifty-nine minutes and twelve seconds, which beat the old record of forty minutes and fifty-nine seconds until Matis blew both times out of the water in the first round of this international world cup.

Minh was very excited. She was wearing a T-shirt I bought for her that depicted Ho Chi Minh with young children sitting around him as he read to them. I had this shirt specially made from an old Vietcong stamp that I had bought on eBay. She was one week late and a little irritable most of the time. But never mean, never mean to me. Just a general irritability that found her grumbling mumbles under her breath. The only thing that brought her relief was a long warm bath. Already a die-hard bath taker, she had now taken it to another level—even taking her meals in the tub.

Dorothy and Towson showed up as the game was about to begin. Towson was accompanying Dorothy more and more to serve as boom operator. Ze looked so pro with headphones and the way ze held the boom pole and mic along ze shoulders like I have seen in behind-the-scenes photos from film sets. Towson said that ze enjoyed doing it because the way we spoke reminded ze of poetry. Ze liked to be able to listen to our every word, isolating each element of speech and language in ze's mind. It was this dialogue between Minh and I that made ze feel warm, ze said. It was the dialogue of two people in sync, and ze knew this from listening to ze's own parents for years and memorizing their dialogue and incorporating it wholesale in ze's poems. When Towson's parents got ze's first book they were very annoyed that Towson had revealed the inner workings of their marriage, but Towson explained that the dialogue of their marriage didn't just belong to them, as it served as a universal trope commenting on the idea of a functioning and largely cohesive union between two people.

"Oooh, I'm so excited!" Minh cried.
"Yes, me too," I said.
"Who are you rooting for?" Minh asked me.
"Who do you think?"
"You better be!"

The announcer introduced the players and then a young Vietnamese woman sang the country's national anthem. Subtitles on the bottom of the screen printed the translation in English.

Soldiers of Vietnam, we go forward,

With the one will to save our Fatherland.
Our hurried steps are sounding on the long and arduous road.
Our flag, red with the blood of victory, bears the
spirit of our
country.
The distant rumbling of the guns mingles with our
marching song.
The path to glory passes over the bodies of our foes.
Overcoming all hardships, together we build our resistance bases.
Ceaselessly for the people's cause we struggle,
Hastening to the battlefield!
Forward! All together advancing!
Our Vietnam is strong and eternal.

"Wow, that's heavy," I said after the singer had concluded.

"Yes. The original lyrics included the line: 'We swear to flay the enemy and drink their blood.'"

"We have the rocket's red glare. But your national anthem takes it up a notch."

Then a young man came onstage and sang the Lithuanian national anthem.

Lithuania, our dear homeland,
Land of worthy heroes!
May your sons draw strength
From your past experiences.

May your children always
Choose the paths of virtue,
May they work towards your good,
And that of all people.

May the sun in Lithuania
Disperse darkness,
And light and truth
May guide our steps.

May love of Lithuania
Burn in our hearts,
In the name of Lithuania,
Unity may blossom!

"That's definitely more gentle. Still, I like the Vietnamese anthem better," I said. "More passion!"

"You got that right! Nobody beats Vietnam. Not the Japanese, not the Chinese, not the French, not the US of A. And certainly not the Lithuanians!"

The people in the auditorium got quiet and we got quiet. Dorothy filmed the screen as the staring contest commenced, and then she turned the camera on us. When you watch a staring contest that could last anywhere from thirty minutes to forty-five minutes or longer you can't help but have your mind start to wander a bit, but it always comes back to the eyes and faces of the players. It is either a split screen of both players or close-ups of the eyes held for long stretches. There is minimal commentary from the announcers. Maybe just some background data such as: "Thanh Nuyguyen was born in the Red River Delta region of Vietnam. She attends Ho Chi Minh City University of Global Studies. She is due to graduate next year. This is her first time competing in an international staring contest but she is already being heralded as one of the best timed starers in the world."

As the clock passed the half-hour mark, one of the announcers said, "Do I detect a smile on Thanh Nuyguyen's face?"

The other announcer responded, "Yes indeed, Thanh Nuyguyen is known for this technique; it has not been determined whether this is a tactic or she is just happy to be competing on the big stage. I imagine maybe a little of both. And by the look of the grimace on Matis's face, he is not appreciating her cheekiness."

In the world of the International Staring Competition smiling was not against the rules, but it was frowned upon by the old guard, of which Mathis was a member. It certainly made it more entertaining to watch and was probably one of the reasons why Thanh was not only a champion but also very popular, in fact a pop star in her own right. That smile, which was not a full-blown smile, and not a Mona Lisa, something in between, something her own, was a reason for her super large following. T-shirts, paintings, emojis, coffee cups, and a thousand other things were adorned with the image of Thanh Nuyguyen's smile. It was reported that there had been an increase in people smiling since the ascendance of Thanh Nuyguyen.

The contest was coming on forty-five minutes. Thanh's smile was in place, yet there was some furrowing in her brows. Matis saw this and very subtly pursed his lips, but it was an avuncular pursing of the lips. He held it for a good two minutes. This inadvertently caused Thanh to loosen up and relax her furrowed brows, and her smile became closer to full-blown, showing the top row of her perfectly aligned, pearly white teeth. Even the announcers took exception: "Do you see that? Thanh Nuyguyen is breaking all decorum with that smile. It is beyond the pale."

"But not against the rules!" Minh said, laughing. "Ah ha ha ha!"

"Look at Matis. He is squinting," I observed.

"Oh my god. You're right, dear. And perspiring."

The announcers repeated what we had observed. "If some of that perspiration gets in his eyes it's all over."

"That's right. The auditorium's temperature is set to sixty-two degrees, as per International Staring Cup regulations."

"It must be the tremendous pressure Thanh Nuyguyen is placing on Matis with her smile."

"Yes, Matis hates emotion of any kind."

"If his squint gets any tighter the judges might call the match for Thanh Nuyguyen."

Over the course of the spectacle, Thanh's smile waned and Matis stopped sweating and squinting. An hour passed. Minh started shifting with sudden movements. "Are you alright, my darling?" I asked her.

"Yes, yes, just terribly uncomfortable. The baby is kicking up a storm."

"Probably senses your excitement."

Thanh's smile was no longer apparent and in fact had turned into a subtle frown. Her eyes, though strong and open, had become sad. I don't know how else to explain it. It was like all of the history of civilization, all of the wars, all of the cruelty, all of the disease and plagues, all of the inequity, racism, oppression, and repression were apparent in her eyes. Meanwhile Matis's eyes were steely and cold. It felt like he had gotten the upper hand, and he knew it. It felt like he was about to crush her.

"My god," Minh cried out, "he's a barbarian!"

Humphrey started barking at the screen. He went near it and snapped his teeth, let out a vicious growl, and then walked away, lying down at Minh's feet.

Towson's arms had gotten tired a while ago and so ze sat down on the ottoman and propped the boom mic between ze legs. Ze was transfixed by the contest. Ze mumbled morosely, "Inhumane." Dorothy had been shooting the whole time. Most of the time I had forgotten that she was there, even though she would pass before us as she filmed our expressions while we watched the contest. She had told me that the camera she had checked out from the film school was quite light. She loved that particular camera because it perfectly replicated the look of the Bolex 16 mm film: the graininess, the chiaroscuro in the contrast of light and dark, and the way it saturated the scene. She continued filming even as Minh began to scream at the screen. "That bastard! He can't get away with it. It's terrible. Terrible what he is doing to Thanh. They need to stop this cruelty. They need to stop this. He is going to make her cry!" she shouted as the tears fell from her eyes. And her screaming at the screen became more strident. "Thanh! Make Matis blink!" And as if Thanh Nuyguyen had heard Minh she broke into a big beautiful smile, a smile that represented more than happiness— it was joy, pure joy, and contentedness, the contentedness of knowing that this life, this moment, was beautiful and safe and this epoch in time was almost a complete realization of the potential benevolence of humanity. Yes, she smiled, the smile of an angel, the smile of a queen. And Matis, like the man whose time had passed, blinked. The announcer cried out, "It's all over!"

Everyone in the room let out a big cry of happiness and joy. And then Minh said, "The baby wants to come out now. The baby wants out." Then her water broke.

CHAPTER 41

◆

Becoming Geronimo Vang wasn't so difficult. Not really. It cost seven hundred and fifty dollars. Cash. There was a place in New Yor's Chinatown that I had overheard some fellows talking about. I was at the Ear Inn listening to jazz on a Sunday night, my weekly routine, and these two guys sitting at the table adjacent to me were discussing the matter.

"Jamie got his new passport on Baxter Street. He must be in Portugal by now."

"No kiddin'?"

"Yeah. Good thing too. Otherwise he'd be dead right now."

"Just like that? Amazing. I'm going to miss that bastard."

"Me too."

"On Baxter Street?"

"Yeah. In the back of a Vietnamese restaurant. You ask for a guy named Lucky. He sets you up. If you've got seven hundred and fifty bucks."

"That all?"

"It's America. It doesn't cost much to become a new person here."

"How do you know all of this?"

"It's a good thing to know. You never know."

So I went down to Baxter Street one spring day with a thousand dollars cash in my pocket. On the corner of Baxter and Bayard was a Vietnamese restaurant called Pho Thin Famous Vietnamese Noodle House. I walked in. It was frenetic. Waiters rushing around, sounds of meat sizzling on the grill, trip-hop music blasting on the sound system; the place was packed with Southeast Asian hipsters and ancient men all wearing dark-blue corduroy jackets. I stopped a waiter and asked for Lucky. He pointed to a door in the back of the restaurant.

I knocked on the door. After a minute I put my ear to the door. I could hear a transistor radio with a sportscaster speaking in Vietnamese. I knocked again. This time louder and repeatedly. The door opened and there was Lucky. He was dressed in a dark-gray three-piece suit, had a cigarette dangling from his mouth, and long black hair that went past his shoulders. He was not tall but exuded height. Giving me the once-over, he then motioned for me to come into his office. I didn't know exactly what to say, so I blurted out, "I have a thousand dollars." I took it out of my pocket and put it on his desk. He went around his desk, sat down and motioned for me to sit down on the chair opposite him. He counted the money. Pulled out five fifties and set them before me. "Only costs seven fifty." He had me stand against a white wall, motioned for me to take off my eyeglasses. He took a photo of me with a digital camera. Next, Lucky went through a door that led to another room. I sat back down. I was to be given a new name, technically a new identity, again. I had been going by the name Joe. Just Joe. It was what people called me, people who wouldn't wait for me to tell them my name when they asked. I didn't have one handy so they called me Joe. After a while I told them unhesitatingly—Joe. And when they asked, "Joe what?" I said, "Joe Harris." Harris was the name of the hat I wore. And all these years, some twenty years I had been Joe Harris. Before that, before I died, a different name. I was substituting one made-up name for another.

It was different this time. This was to be my real name. Officially. To get a driver's license, a bank account, credit cards, a lease, and so forth. The name I would use to book airline flights to foreign countries. With this name I would start sending out my manuscript. It would be the name my book would be published under. And I knew that it would be published. Don't ask me how I knew it but I did. I guess I knew it because I knew that it was good. It wasn't arrogance. I had read enough books to know this. And I had connections from the bookstore. When they told me that they thought my name was Joe Harris, I would tell them that Joe Harris wasn't my real name. My real name is . . .

"Geronimo Vang." I looked down at the passport, and there was my picture, and the name next to it was Geronimo Vang. I said it again. "Geronimo Vang. Yes. It's a funny name. But life is funny." I thanked Lucky and walked out of Pho Thin Famous Vietnamese Noodle House and into the air that suffused Baxter Street. The air that was New York City. And the funny thing was, I felt like Geronimo Vang. I looked at myself in the windows of the stores on the street as I strolled. Yep, there was Geronimo Vang. It's official. I am Geronimo Vang. And now my child has my last name, which is Minh's last name. We are the Vang family of Ditmas Park. And when he or she or ze or it is older the name can be changed to whatever name that person cares to be.

CHAPTER 42

◆

"**S**hould I stop filming?!" Dorothy said, still holding the camera to her face.

I looked to Minh, who shook her head. "No, don't stop filming."

"I'll pull out the car. Take you to the hospital!" I said in a panic.

"No time!" Minh cried out as if someone had just punched her in the gut.

"Get a sheet from the bed and lay it on the floor," Minh said to me. Her face was calm but her eyes were filled with a hundred worries. But not debilitatingly so.

I nodded and ran upstairs. I went into the closet of our bedroom and grabbed a forest green Brooklinen bedsheet. I passed the mirror as I crossed the room. I stopped for a second to observe myself, "Geronimo Vang."

I laid the sheet on the floor in front of the sofa. Towson propped the boom mic against the coffee table and helped me to lay Minh down on the sheet. She was breathing heavily. Deep breaths through her nose, exhaling through her mouth, like we had read in Ina May Gaskin's book *Spiritual Midwifery*. We had no intention of having a home birth and had made plans at a very reputable and expensive birthing center in Park Slope. Some of the literature around midwifery and home births was beautiful and interesting and the new drugs that made birth painless yet allowed one to be fully present for it were too good to be true. All of that seemed to be out the window.

Towson sat behind Minh. I was at her front, on my knees,

ready to retrieve the baby, and it happened so fast that there was nothing to think about. It happened so fast, and the baby came right into my hands, and the baby was pink and glistening. And the baby cried out immediately and I realized that I had stopped hearing sound until I heard the baby cry. The baby looked up at me, stopped crying, and made the most intense eye contact that I had ever experienced. Her eyes were dark brown and on her head was a mass of dark hair. Her mouth closed with what seemed to me a slight smile. "Dad, she is having a staring contest with you!" Dorothy said. Everyone laughed.

I came out of the moment, turned around and handed the baby to Minh who, with tears pouring down her face, clutched the baby to her breast and said something quietly in Vietnamese.

Dorothy went in closer to film the baby nuzzling with Minh. "Geronimo," Towson said, "you must go and get something to cut the umbilical cord with." I rose and again ran upstairs into our bedroom, passing the mirror, the shadow vapor of my image passing, and into the adjoining bathroom. The bathroom which was the one place we lavished not a small number of resources. Nothing extraordinary, just an Italian white marble floor, Duravit toilet and sink, a steam shower, and a large rectangular bathtub with perfect lighting for reading. The bathtub was both Minh's and my favorite place to read, and we designed the whole room with that in mind. At one point it was her vision to give birth there, until I convinced her to do it at the birthing center in Park Slope. I was adamantly squeamish at the idea of a home birth.

On the ledge of the sink was my stainless steel safety razor. The same one that I had been using since I got to New York City. The same one I used to shave from my face the disgusting ropelike, matted, blood-orange sweaty beard. Not the same blade of course, but the same instrument. And from this same German safety razor I had once unscrewed the knob from the bottom of the device, the lids open on either side to expose the double-edged blade, and with that blade, on more than one-more than one hundred occasions- I had contemplated opening my veins. There had been no compelling reason not to. There had been nobody who loved me in this world. Nobody who would miss me. But even with this in mind at the time, for some reason I found life enjoyable enough to continue with it. I rotated the knob at the bottom of the device and retrieved from it the brand-new blade which I had inserted that very same morning, the last one in the drawer, making a mental note to buy more at the convenience store.

I walked briskly out of the bathroom, passing the mirror, stopping only for a split second to look at myself, to say my name, "Geronimo," see those eyes, see that mouth, see those hands, see the room, the bed where the baby was made, this is happening, it is all happening. I walked out of the room and briskly down the stairs and into the living room. I got down on my knees, grabbed the umbilical cord which dangled from the baby's belly, curling its way back to the inside of Minh, and I cut it, unhesitatingly, I cut it. "Now you must deliver the placenta, my darling," I told Minh.

CHAPTER 43

◆

The placenta came out on its own accord only moments after the baby was born. With both hands I took it to the kitchen, placed it in a freezer-friendly Ziploc bag, wrote on the bag using a marker, "Beautiful Baby Vang's placenta," and placed it in the freezer. Towson helped Minh onto the sofa and propped her up with pillows while I wrapped the baby in the swaddling cloth. We had purchased the swaddling cloth at the birthing center when we visited to book services. I handed Minh the newborn expertly wrapped. I must have watched the video on how to do it fifty times.

"What are you going to call it?" Towson asked.

"It? Not it. And not ze. Her for now. Later she can tell us to change it to ze or he or whatever pronoun she prefers. I am just going to do what is most comfortable for me right now. But I can adapt. As far as a name, I was thinking Thanh. Geronimo? What do you think?"

"I think that's fine. That's a fine name. We have time to let her tell us if that's okay with her."

"Yes. She will tell us. She will tell us everything. Look at those eyes."

"You were so brave to let me film you," Dorothy said with the camera held to her face, still filming.

"Was I? Can you be brave if there is no forethought?"

"Maybe that's the definition of bravery," I said.

I looked at Minh, and there was so much ease in her demeanor, as if she had just finished a workout as opposed to giving birth. Such a casual acceptance of new life and the life we had known being amended. The power intrinsic in her was haughty and redundant.

"What was it like?" Towson asked. "How did it feel?"

"At first it is like really bad period cramps. Then it becomes like a pounding, like someone knocking on the door wanting in, or out. And in fact that is what it is. The odd thing was that I stopped hearing sound when the pounding began. I saw your faces and your concern. I saw your movements but no accompanying sound. I knew that I was moaning or crying but I could hear nothing. I could feel, and what I felt is impossible to explain. The physical quality. At least for now. It was like dying, I think. Dying and going to a higher plane. Then, upon coming back, it was as if an orchestra had just played a crescendo; sound and life were back again. The knowledge that everything had changed. Not just our lives, all life. Everywhere."

The days passed. Dorothy and Towson came over every day to film how we were coping. The neighbors also came by daily, each family on the block bringing a casserole or a pot of spaghetti, pies and cakes and cooked vegetables and fresh-baked bread. Seemed like each family had a master chef. They came to make sure we were alright and they came to see the baby. Word had spread about this baby's eyes. Each person wanted to have a staring contest with her. After a week Towson became gatekeeper; ze now turned most people away, saying that Minh needed her rest. Which she did. Oddly Minh never complained about the attention. I think she was amazed by it and wanted to know what was behind it. Was the baby a phenomenon or was this just what it was like when you gave birth? Everyone becomes nicer and communities become closer with new life.

Minh and I became closer. If that was possible. We shared in our reverie, trading glances, knowing smiles, knowing that we had been through so much already, so much experience, and now this event which made every moment leading up to the new moment a sanctified prelude. Minh would whisper-sing to Thanh from William Blake's *Songs of Innocence and Experience*:

Little Lamb who made thee?
Dost thou know who made thee?
Gave thee life and bid thee feed
By the stream and o'er the mead;
Gave thee clothing of delight,
Softest clothing wooly bright;
Gave thee such a tender voice,
Making all the vales rejoice:
Little Lamb who made thee?
Dost thou know who made thee?

"You made thee," I whispered back to Minh. "No," she replied, "The universe, through us, made thee." And this made us laugh. We did the same routine throughout the day. Eventually Thanh would giggle when Minh began, at the words *Little lamb*.

At first the baby slept in bed with us even though we were both not wanting to practice fashionable attachment parenting. We wanted to protect our bond, our intimacy. Not just sexually speaking, but also our intense camaraderie. It proved difficult to keep Thanh in her crib, especially since Minh was nursing so often. And it never ceased to amaze us to look down at that tawny-skinned being, with almond eyes and cathartic hair, her perfect little nibs of fingers and toes and dimpled arms and legs, soft like a satin tube of down glowing like a cherub in a painting by Bouguereau, to know that it was from our love that she came. In time she would go to her crib, yet not at first, and we would always keep her near at night. At least until she was two years of age. That was our plan.

PART FOUR

CHAPTER 44

◆

When Thanh was six months everything happened all at once. Dorothy's documentary of Minh and I had its premiere at the Paris Theater, my novel came out, and Minh's anime television streaming series of her book about the Vietnamese Super Girl Hero was first aired. All on the same day.

I was upstairs putting on my tuxedo. Minh came in as I was struggling with the bow tie. Just like on our wedding day, I insisted on using a real bow tie, not a clip-on. And just like on our wedding day, I was having difficulty. "You'll get it," she said, patting me on the back. We looked at ourselves in the mirror. She looked radiant in her black satin dress, necklace of small white pearls, long black gloves. She left the room to go to her study to meditate before we were to leave. I went over to Thanh's crib to check on her. She was down for a nap. Sometimes you'd look in there and she'd just be sitting quietly with her eyes open, just staring into the air or looking at something that I couldn't see. At this moment she was soundly sleeping. Dorothy and Towson were downstairs having coffee. Humphrey was in the backyard chasing squirrels. The doorbell rang and I could hear Towson's heavy and determined steps going to answer it. Then throughout the house was heard a gargantuan sigh; it sounded like a strong gust of wind. We all knew it was Towson's and we all knew what it meant.

Shirley's chatter, heard through the floorboards, sounded like a box of finches. Minh came into our bedroom, her eyes wide, and for the first time in a few days the baby began to cry. Minh took her from the crib and put her to her breast to nurse. "Well," she said, "I guess it was inevitable. You better go down to, you know, surmise the situation." She looked a little flummoxed. I could see her inner process calming her nerves, her mind at work, her letting the peaceful powers of the universe soothe her psyche.

I went downstairs. Sitting on the ottoman in the living room, dressed in a purple, orange, and yellow tie-dye dress, clear plastic high heels, and with a halo of plastic daisies attached to her head, as if she had just come from Woodstock, was Shirley. The hippy style had come back in vogue, as is the cycle with fashion, regurgitating earlier styles, because in reality there was a finite supply of ideas when it came to everything; all art was just a matter of how you reintegrated the elements. I still wore only suits, Minh wore stylish yet somewhat conservative dresses, skirts, and blouses. Towson and Dorothy often wore T-shirts adorned with photos of new wave bands from the 1980s.

Shirley rose to greet me. "What an exciting day," she exclaimed. It seemed that she already had a few drinks under her belt. She was ebullient, truly, but as always she emitted an air of danger. I went over and she took hold of my upper arms, looked at me. I gave her a slight embrace and then a kiss on either cheek as the French do. It wasn't necessarily my idea to do this, she sort of guided me. "You look well," I said obligingly. "Thank you, kind sir. I am just thrilled to be here to see my darling daughter's work. And congratulations to you for the publication of your latest novel." I imagined that she had yet to read it, as it had only been made public that day, and I wondered, when she did read it, how she would process it. I wondered if perhaps I had overstated in my mind how potentially explosive it was.

My agent didn't think of it as anything other than a good piece of fiction. He was happy with it, as was the publishing house. They probably didn't realize how in many ways it was autofiction and thus a confession. It told the story of Minh and myself, our love affair, and the book wove throughout this narrative the backstory of how the protagonist had died and been reborn, losing all recollection of his life before his fatal drug overdose. Of how he found his way to New York City, got a job at a used bookstore. And how, with the help of books and records and of the city itself and all of the characters who inhabited it, he created an identity, a new identity. How so many of us come to this city almost a blank slate and become the person we want to be. You get chopped down, dissected, but there's always an opportunity to make your way back together. And then a daughter from his former life appears. She informs him of his previous identity and his possible involvement in the murder of her stepfather. His erratic, volatile, alcoholic ex-wife/widow comes to town, and that is when everything is threatened, all the happiness and prosperity that he and his wife had manifested. And just as quickly, after an embarrassing episode at Coney Island, the threat from the ex-wife/widow is abated. She leaves. And the man and his daughter grow closer while the man and his wife's idyllic life continues, culminating with the birth of a daughter. Another daughter for him. It is all there, with a lot of digressions about literature and philosophy, maybe boring for some, but for the bookish a way to hold interest against the exigencies of a fantastical story.

She sat on the ottoman in the living room. Legs crossed. "I loved it," Shirley said as she took a sip from the glass of white port I had poured her. "Your novel that is."

"You read it already?" I asked.

"Bought a copy at the airport and read it on the flight here."

"And you loved it?"

"I did. Such an incredible story. Had me holding my breath."

"How do you mean?"

"I was rapt, I mean, with what will happen to the little family. The reunion with the daughter was so touching."

"Mom, stop playing games," Dorothy chimed while sitting next to Towson on the sofa, their hands clenched together.

"What games?"

"What are you going to do?"

"In response to?"

"Shirley," I said, "we all know that this novel is a confession of sorts."

"A coming clean? As the title of the novel goes."

"Yes. Quite literally."

"No, not literally. Because it is literary. It is a novel. So it is fiction."

"True enough."

"So you are protected."

"Protected from what?"

"From the truth."

"What is the truth?"

"Nobody knows."

"One person knows," Minh said as she entered the room holding Thanh.

CHAPTER 45

◆

At first things went well, the baby latched on, there was no engorgement or any breastfeeding issues. And even though the baby woke Minh and myself throughout the night we weren't too haggard. I stayed up with Minh while she tended to the baby and was in charge of changing her diapers since Minh had to do the work of feeding her. But then, about six weeks after Thanh was born, Minh started falling into a depression.

We were both aware that postpartum depression was something that happened at varying levels. We thought we were prepared. I made sure that she had all of the things that brought her comfort: Fuji apples, Asian pears, bacon, turmeric tea, hot chocolate with whipped cream, churros, pho, ramen, bath salts, classical music, foot rubs, cuddling, trashy TV shows, art house cinema, design magazines—actually all of the things that were part of our daily existence before Thanh, which now I tried to anticipate, before Minh actually craved for them. Yet, she started falling and we knew that there was nothing we could do about it until we saw how and which way the fall happened.

It was subtle, at first, mostly languid moping and feigned smiles. And then the chronic naps that matched Thanh's started. Basically they were both getting almost twenty hours of sleep a day. Minh napped a lot during her pregnancy – now she took it to another level. Humphrey was only too happy to join in and provide another warm body. Dorothy and Towson became very concerned. Every time they came over Minh was asleep. They did usually come over at prime napping time—4 p.m.

Still, it was worrisome. I have to admit that I became annoyed as well. Where was my partner, my companion, my lover, my best friend? I knew that I was being incredibly selfish, yet I felt abandoned.

I stumbled across a quote from Walt Whitman's *Guide to Manly Health and Training.*

The healthy sleep—the breathing sleep and regular—the unbroken and profound repose—the night as it passes soothing and renewing the whole frame. Yes, nature surely keeps her choicest blessings for the slumber of health—and nothing short of that can ever know what true sleep is.

And then I fell into Minh and the baby's routine and napped along with them. It was good that I had finished my novel during the pregnancy, except for the birth of the baby chapter. Minh had signed off on her deal and had approved the script for the series. So our work was done, and in a sense we were entitled to a respite. And we took it. Only waking to go to the bathroom and bathe and order food, some light yoga, walk Humphrey, and then back to sleep. Still there remained a cloud of darkness around Minh.

"What's it like?" I asked her earnestly.

"I don't know. It's hard to explain. Mostly I feel loss. A sense of loss. Which is ridiculous since I have only gained, not lost. The pregnancy was smooth, as smooth and beautiful as I could have ever imagined. Our life is really ideal. I am doing the work I want to do when I want to do it. The baby is perfect and you are as loving a husband as I could imagine. I know that my mom would find me absurd. She and my father struggled through the dire conditions of the American war and she worked from nothing to become a success in her business and a renowned poet. That's why I don't tell her about what I am going through. Which actually doesn't help."

"Maybe you could try her. She might surprise you."

"Maybe."

"Is it that you feel that you have lost the life we had before?"

"I thought about that. And no. That's not it. More like I lost a part of me."

"I understand."

"No, you don't. You can't."

"I guess so."

"Oh my love. Come here. Don't worry. It will pass."

But it got worse. Minh started having intense crying jags. We would wake from a long nap. The baby would be fussing to have her diaper changed and then be fed. After she was fed and changed, and after laying her down, we would engage in a staring contest which she inevitably won. One day, I had her on my knee. I got her to laugh by making funny faces. There is nothing like a baby to make you act like an idiot. And there is nothing more joyous than a baby's laugh. I looked around to see if Minh was seeing this. I heard her in the bathroom sobbing. Increasing in volume and then subsiding. Then I heard the bathtub running. After putting the baby in the crib I went in and lit candles while she sat in the tub. I'd turned down the lights. I went downstairs and put on a Morton Feldman record, which ran through speakers connected to the bedroom. I tried to normalize whatever it was that she was going through by placing it in the context of how we lived our lives thus letting Minh know that she was supported, completely. I hoped that this would help but sometimes it seemed like she would never come out of the sadness.

This went on for a few weeks. Time lost importance. It was slippery. When you sleep not only at night but through the day, time bends.

Then, coinciding with the baby's newfound mobility, her crawling around on the ground like a little tortoise, it seemed to be the impetus for an awakening for Minh. She started keeping regular hours, and as always, I aligned with her. We woke in the morning, cuddled, looked into each other's eyes, smiled, kissed, and then both of us would go over to the crib, look at her sleeping quietly and then make our way downstairs for coffee and to peruse the paper or a magazine like *The New Yorker* or the *New York Review of Books* and make pleasant conversation about the items we were reading or the events around town that we would like to take in but probably wouldn't. Just like that, we were back. Only, we had a charge now. A little human being that was now the most important thing in our lives. Not our relationship, or our work, this human being. And we were thoroughly and completely alright with that.

CHAPTER 46

◆

"So that's where it happened, in front of the sofa."

"How did you know that?" Minh shot back. She looked at Dorothy, who shrugged her shoulders.

"She probably got that from my book," I said, sheepishly.

"From your book?" Minh said cuttingly. I had never heard her speak this way to me before.

"Haven't you read it?" Shirley inquired of Minh toyingly.

"I was a little busy. But it's fine. I just didn't know. Yes, it happened right there," Minh said, regaining her composure and pointing to the front of the sofa with her one free hand, the other holding a sleeping Thanh. She said to Shirley, "Your daughter's support was invaluable."

"Not just my daughter. Your daughter too," Shirley said, looking at me with a wry smile on her face. "And besides, all she did was film it. Is that going to be in the movie tonight?"

"Mom," Dorothy said. "I appreciate you renting out the theater for me, and for coming to support the premiere, but please, try to be pleasant."

"What?! I am being pleasant. I'm just making conversation. No, that's not true. You're right. I'm being confrontational, but, you have to admit, it is a dramatic revelation, that which is contained in *Coming Clean*. Very brave of you to write it as such, Geronimo. Or Gerald. Oh wait, that's the old you. The you that died. And this new you is ever so different. Although, it is not like you actually died. They call it near-death. A near-death experience."

"His heart stopped and he was pronounced dead. According

to the state and the world, that person, that Gerald Hopson, is dead. And another person came to, completely, with no knowledge of a previous life," Minh said, almost shouting.

"That is, until his daughter came and clued him in. But, I'm not trying to make waves. Your depiction of me, or the character who resembles me, is a little offensive, but you make me out to be perhaps more glamorous and flamboyant then I really am. I'm not bothered by that. I could be, but I am not. And so I just want to say, I am not going to make waves. I will continue going on being your widow. Though, technically, are we still married?"

Towson spoke, "I thought you said that you were not going to make waves."

"Oh Towson, that's what I said. Although, your poem entitled "Make Waves" is one of my favorites of yours. And you delivered it so powerfully at the inauguration. I guess you meant it more in a political sense."

"Why does everything you say sound like a threat?" Towson said almost to zeself.

"I am not threatening anyone. Let me be clear. This is who I am. No filter. Right? Let's just enjoy and celebrate this great day, this great night. That's all I am here for."

Shirley's phone chimed. She pulled it from her little fanny pack that matched her hippy dress.

"Oh great! The limousine is here!"

"Limousine?" Dorothy uttered incredulously.

"Yes of course, my darling daughter. It's the world premiere. One must attend in style and class. After all, this is the Paris Theater. Same theater where John Cassavetes held the premiere for his first film *Shadows*. Of course, his premiere was an unmitigated disaster. I'm sure your premiere will be more successful."

"Oh Mom," Dorothy said, a little excited at the prospect of riding in a limousine. "I've never been in one. What do you say, Towson?"

"I rode in one at the inauguration," Towson said drolly.

"Then what are we waiting for? Come on, Geronimo and Minh. Let's do this. Family style."

I looked at Minh, who burst out laughing. She sat down on the arm of the sofa.

"Thank you so much for the offer," I said to Shirley. "I think we will take my car. It has a car seat for the baby, and I think, well, it will be better."

"Oh yes. Of course. No worries, my dearies. Just let me freshen up." Shirley went to the bathroom down the hall from the living room.

Towson and Dorothy put on their coats. "We'll wait outside. See you there," Dorothy said. She and Towson went out through the front door. Minh moved herself to the sofa proper. I sat down next to her and took ahold of her hand. Thanh woke and stirred. Minh pulled her hand away from mine, unbuttoned the top of her dress, and put Thanh to her breast. Thanh's little hands played with Minh's pearls and made eye contact with me. She seemed to sense my stress and gave me a comforting smile.

"Are you mad at me?"

"Whatever for?"

"Writing about, about, you know, writing about . . ."

"Of course not. Oh, maybe a little, but you told me that you were going to, and even if I didn't read it, well, you told me you were going to. My goodness, after all, I let Dorothy film it and, well, you know, I am sort of an introvert . . ."

"I know, so am I."

"No, you're a recluse. There's a difference."

"True."

"And don't always agree with me."

"But. You're right."

"No, I'm not. I am not always right."

"Usually."

"Are you being snide?"

"No! I mean it. That's why, no, that's not why."

"Why what?"

"Why I love you. But not why. Entirely."

"Yes, well. I know. The thing is, as I was saying. I am introverted, but, but, if art is life and life is art then you must compel yourself to embody it. To strip away the veneer. You showed me that. You are the brave one. You are right. Not always, but at your core, you are right. And now, with Thanh, she will be able to see. All of it. And that is only a good thing. Despite any discomfort I might feel."

"Well, we can agree to agree."

She laughed. Thanh laughed too. And then I laughed.

Shirley reemerged from the bathroom. "They're outside, waiting for you," I told her. My voice flat, almost somber. I noticed that some strands of hair dangling down from her crown of plastic daisies were gray or white. It was then, for some reason, caused by those few strands of hair, I felt real compassion for Shirley. And I felt ashamed that it was the first time I had. If I had loved her at one point, was it possible to unlove her? I didn't know. I honestly didn't know.

She grimaced at me and Minh, and put her hands on her hips. "We will see you at the Paris Theater. There will be a Q and A after. Will you participate?"

"I think not," Minh said. "But thank you. So generous of you to rent out the theater."

She smiled humanely and said, "She's my little girl. Well, now, she's my young woman."

Shirley looked at me. I felt that she was going to say "*She's yours, too.*" But she just chuckled and walked out the front door.

CHAPTER 47

◆

The theater was filled. Mostly friends of Dorothy's and Towson's from NYU and fans of Minh's books. Maybe a curious smattering from my readership, and members of the press, mostly women. Unlike Cassavetes's first-cut screening of *Shadows*, the audience did not walk out in droves. In fact they were enraptured. Dorothy used various filters and cinematic techniques to convey the harmony and/or tension between Minh and myself, creating a kaleidoscope of color, image, sound, and words to tell our story, the story of the nine months that she filmed us. It showed, even demonstrated, how a couple can handle the stress of a creative and romantic life in the build-up to the birth of a child. Mostly it was Minh's story, I was just a supporting actor. And she was presented heroically. Culminating in the delivery of her child on the floor of our living room. I watched the film feeling like a spectator. I forgot that it was me on the screen. At the end of the film the crowd erupted in applause and wouldn't stop until Minh stood and took a bow.

Four stools were brought out and set before the screen. Shirley walked in front of them holding a wireless microphone. "Good evening. What a film. I am the producer of the film and Dorothy's mother." The crowd gave a vigorous round of applause. I looked to Minh. She smiled and shook her head. "Should we leave?" I asked her. "Absolutely."

Sitting midway from the screen and at the end of a row, we rose to leave. Shirley exclaimed, "And there they are. The lovely stars of Dorothy's film. Let's give them a round of applause and perhaps they, with Dorothy, will answer some of your questions."

I found myself on one of those stools in front of the screen, sitting next to Minh who had a wide-awake Thanh reclining upright in a sling and was sitting next to Dorothy who was sitting next to Shirley. Each one of us holding a wireless microphone. "So, let me ask a few questions and then we can turn it over to the audience who I am sure have some questions of their own. Dorothy, what inspired you to make this film?"

"Well, as Picabia said, 'I want to open the eyes of those who have the same eyes as mine to make them believe in the eyes I have myself.'"

"Who has the same eyes as you?"

"Well, as Picabia said, 'Apples fall from trees to sow other apples which also fall from trees in the hope that these apples will become stars like the sun which makes apples grow.'"

"An apple doesn't fall far from the tree."

"Unless there is a strong wind."

"A very strong wind."

"What is your favorite Picabia quote?"

"'Children are the penitence for love.' But you know that."

"You like Picabia a lot, it seems."

"Yes."

"A more nuts-and-bolts kind of question: how long did it take you to make this wonderful film?"

"It took nine months to shoot and three months to edit."

"Incredible. And was it hard to convince Geronimo and Minh to participate?"

"Um. No, not really. They like Picabia too."

"Let me ask them for myself. Minh. Do you like Picabia?"

"Yes. Though I have never read him, I just heard Dorothy quote him."

"Why did you let her make this film?"

"What do you mean?"

"Why did you let this young woman come into your house and film you and your 'husband' (Shirley used her fingers to indicate quotes) day after day. I would think it would feel very invasive?"

"Yes, at first, however, Dorothy and Towson, who did the sound, managed to make themselves like the proverbial flies on the wall. I felt that it was a wonderful opportunity for many reasons. One of them being that Dorothy asked; so it was nice to say yes to someone who you love and admire."

"You love my daughter?"

"Yes, of course."

"And Geronimo. Do you love my daughter as well?"

"Yes."

"Maybe that is because she is your daughter as well."

"Yes."

"And having made this film, having participated in the making of this film, in fact being the subject of this film, and then seeing yourself and your wife on the big screen, has that altered your perception of yourself and your world?"

"Yes. How could it not? Every day there is always something, or many things that do that, if your eyes are open."

"And what about the fact that Dorothy came to you with the truth about yourself?"

"Yes. I am grateful to her for many reasons."

"It's all in your new novel, *Coming Clean*."

"Yes."

"Let me ask you this. Did you kill Dorothy's stepfather, my husband?"

"No."

"Not the you that is before us but the you that was before, before your near-death experience."

"Death experience."

"Whatever."

"The answer is no."

"How do you know if you can't remember?"

"Because you did. I think."

"That's a laugh."

"Well, didn't you?"

"I don't remember. I was quite drunk and on drugs that night."

"Either way the case is closed and that's that."

"Well, here is another bit of news from your past life. You are still married to me, thus making your marriage to Minh null and void. As well as her US citizenship."

"That would be true if we had actually been married. Unfortunately, or fortunately, the wedding officiant you hired never sent in the paperwork. I have a feeling he did as instructed."

"Damn! That's true. Well, let's open this bad boy to the audience. And tell your baby to quit staring at me."

CHAPTER 48

◆

I slept heavily. Like bricks. Minh and I made love, not the first time since the child had come, but the first time, the first time we forgot ourselves in the act of making love. Touch, simple, kiss, caress, intuitive, penetrate, absorb, unity, oneness, ecstasy, relinquish, carnal, exhaust, resume, rejuvenate, resuscitate, reclaim, recondite, enigmatic, relish, pacify, breathe, breathlessness, explode, matter, angular, moist, succulent, contour, contort, object, subject, proclaim, elevate, saturate, profligate, hypnotic, trip-notic, cathartic, embark, tantric, postulate, semen, seed, prostatic, secretion, inroad, outerelement, sweat, tears; everything reduced to propitious solitude.

I smelled fire, I sensed smoke. It was hard to lift myself; so deep was I in sleep. I rose and felt the heat that came from the curtains in our room, on fire. The baby's crib was near enough to the curtains that I was sure that it was about to go up in flames. I jumped out of bed stark naked and as I did Minh let out a bloodcurdling scream. By the time I got to the crib the fire had caught the rug, a white fluffy rug which the crib sat upon. Thanh had pulled herself up and held onto the side of the crib, her eyes had terror in them, which to me was worse than the fire.

"Something is burning," Minh said.

I opened my eyes, "No kidding," I murmured.

The white fluffy rug and the baby's crib were fine. There was something burning downstairs.

I walked downstairs, still naked. The smell of smoke came

from the kitchen. I went in and found that the curtain above the kitchen sink was on fire. I grabbed the fire extinguisher and put out the fire. How was it possible that the curtain above the sink, where there was no source of heat, could have caught on fire? The window was open, which was unusual. We usually kept that window closed and locked, not that we were afraid of burglary, but if someone wanted that would be the easiest point of entry. And what about the fire alarm? I went to check it above on the opposite wall. The battery was missing.

Upstairs I found Minh nursing Thanh. She laughed at me and I looked down at myself and realized I must have looked a little silly stark naked. I got into bed. "What was it?" she asked calmly.

"The kitchen curtains were on fire."

"Oh my goodness. How could that have happened?"

"I don't know. The only obvious explanation was that somebody lit it. The window was open."

Minh gestured for me to get into bed. I did and moved close to her. I looked down at Thanh whose eyes locked into mine. She smiled, this made me blink. She blinked three times, very slowly. I tilted my head like a dog. This made her giggle.

"She wouldn't do that, would she?" Minh asked listlessly.

"I wouldn't put it past her," I said as if I were reading from a script.

"And the battery was gone from the smoke alarm,"

Minh opened her eyes wide, "Jesus Christ!"

"I had just changed the batteries last week. First of the month as per usual."

"Maybe you forgot to put in the new one when you took out the old."

"No, I've never done that. She went to the bathroom, when we were on the sofa. She could have done it then."

"I suppose. Though. If she wanted to burn down the house she could have tried a little harder."

"Probably drunk. Should we call the cops?" I asked Minh with not much resolution.

"I don't know. Let's see what Dorothy says. She and Towson

are coming for breakfast."

We tried to go back to sleep but it was not possible. So, we sat up and read until sunlight filled the room. I went downstairs to make coffee. First I pulled down what was left of the curtain, threw it in the trash, and then cleaned up the area around the sink as best I could. As the Coffee Master was percolating I heard someone come through the front door. "Oh my god. What the hell happened?" Dorothy shouted as she entered the kitchen.

"So, tell me," Minh said, taking a sip of her coffee then placing it back down on the arm of the wicker chair on the front porch, "was your mother back at your apartment when we dropped you off?"

"No, she wasn't. But she came a short time after that."

"And she was drunk," Towson spat, sitting next to Dorothy on the swing.

"That's not terribly surprising," I said, leaning against the banister, holding a sleeping Thanh in a sling wrapped over my shoulder.

"She was pissed that we didn't go back with her in the limo. But she didn't say much else. And she had a bottle of champagne which she carried with her into our bedroom, which is where she was sleeping."

"Where did you guys sleep?" I asked solicitously.

"On the goddamn floor," Towson said angrily.

"And was she there when you left this morning?" Minh asked.

"Yes. I stuck my head in to check and see if she was alright."

"And was she?" I asked.

"She was still fully dressed, her arms and legs akimbo, and she was murmuring."

"Could you hear what she was saying?" Minh said.

"A little. She was saying your name," and Dorothy pointed to me.

"She was saying Geronimo's name?" Minh asked.

"Yes. No. She was saying his other name. She was saying

Gerald. She was saying 'I'm sorry, Gerald.'"

"Sorry for what, I wonder," I thought out loud.

"I don't know. But it is the first time I ever heard her apologize. Even if it was just a dream."

"Probably sorry for setting, or trying to set, our house on fire," Minh said angrily.

Thanh started to stir and so I gently bounced her up and down.

"We don't know for certain that it was her," I said.

Everybody looked at me and made a moaning sound.

"I know my mother, and if she is one thing, she is vindictive. To the core. The look on her face when I told her that we were not going back with her in the limousine was deadly."

"Why is she so angry?" I asked innocently.

"She hates to be fooled. More than anything. And she thinks you made a fool of her. I'm not saying you did. You only did what you needed to do. To survive and thrive. I'm so glad I found you. You are a good person, Dad, and I am sure that you have always been a good person."

"That's where you're wrong, my darling daughter." It was Shirley, standing on the pathway to the front porch near the steps.

"Yes, that's where you are wrong. Not only was he not a good person, he was a fucking bastard."

CHAPTER 49

◆

Shirley staggered up the steps to the porch holding onto the handrail for support. Her hair was unkempt, makeup around her eyes smeared, her black strapless dress askew—it looked as though it had been put on backward, which it had. She moved towards Minh and sat down in the empty chair next to her.

"Mom, you look terrible. What happened to you?" Dorothy said, abjectly concerned.

"I walked here. All the way from the East Village. Quite a walk. You know, the East Village in the morning is like walking the halls of a mental asylum. Believe me, I know. I saw such desperate people, people literally howling like wounded dogs, or incantating to God like Job.

But then you get to Brooklyn, and it is so quiet. The downtown and through the quaint streets of Cobble Hill, Carroll Gardens, Park Slope, Windsor Terrace, sounds like Wales these names. And Ditmas Park. My god. Such enchantment. And look at this, gathered together on your porch, Geronimo—just the simple picture of twenty-first century domesticity."

"Mom, let me get you some water."

"No! I don't want any fucking water."

"You look ill."

"I am ill. Ill with betrayal."

"That's silly, Mom. I have not betrayed you. Even if you did it. I will love you."

"Did what?"

"Set my kitchen on fire," Minh said laconically.

"Fuck off. I don't know what you are talking about."

"Listen, Shirley," I said, "I know that you think . . ."

"You don't know what I think, Geronimo. What a stupid fucking name. You don't know anything. You don't know. You pretend dumb. Maybe you are dumb, maybe you don't remember. But I do. I remember. And you were not some innocent who I broke. Who I was unfaithful to and left to heartache. You were a drug addict and a drunk and you were an abusive asshole. You never hit me outright, but you tortured me daily with venomous words. Like it was a sport of some kind. It is true that right before Dorothy was born, and for a while after, you got cleaned up. And then you were a different person, with her, a different person, and I had hope. But you started with drugs again and I got the fuck out. Thank god for Antonio. He was a drunk too, but at least he was a happy drunk."

As she spoke, sensations and images started flashing through my mind. I felt possessed by something, by another entity, by another personality, as if I were becoming another person, and I felt different, and I felt a darkness, and the sense of succumbing to a void. And an impulse to do, if not evil, then to do grossly selfish behavior. The baby shifted in the sling and I snapped out of it.

"Geronimo? Are you alright?" Minh asked of me.

"Geronimo! Always alright, Geronimo. Fictitious being that he is. In fact, always has been. You don't know. But he was handsome, and dashing, and a grifter and a rickroller. I lied when I said he never hit me. He hit me once. But that's okay, I hit him first. Sucker-punched him. He was just standing there, in the kitchen, wavering like a flag on a flagpole, and I came up and with my fist crushed his cheek. He staggered, regained his balance, and then slapped me hard across the face. But he didn't go any further. He could have, but he didn't."

"Mom, settle down. What's the point of all of this? Let it lie, let it lie. Remember what Picabia said: 'A bird teaches a fish to swim, without hatred and without bitterness.'"

Shirley stopped. She looked at her daughter, smiled.

I felt like I was watching a movie, I wanted popcorn, I craved popcorn.

"I'm going to go and make some popcorn," I said.

"For breakfast?" Minh asked.

"No, yes."

Everyone looked at me as if I were falling ill. I gave Thanh to Minh and walked into the house. Humphrey followed me. The light was diffused in the house, the air still and semi-dark. In the kitchen I pulled down a large, shiny All-Clad stock pot, poured in some olive oil, put in half a stick of butter and turned the heat on medium-high. After the butter had melted I dropped in the popcorn seeds. Sounded like pebbles. I looked down at Humphrey who was staring at me expectantly. I felt a tap on my shoulder. I turned around. It was Shirley. She slapped me hard across the face. "Now we're even."

I rubbed my cheek. "Not technically. If what you are saying is true, you hit me first."

"So, not even?"

A popcorn popped, and then another; soon it sounded like hail on a tin roof.

"We're even if you say we're even."

"Did anyone ever tell you that you are quite insipid?"

"I don't think so." I put on oven mitts and started shaking the pot.

"No, they wouldn't."

"The anger . . ."

"The irrational nature of my anger fascinates me. Does it fascinate you too?"

"As a matter of fact it does."

"It gives me an aura, yes?"

"That it does. Though it is quite disconcerting."

"Most of the time I can barely conceal it."

"I know. Do you want to not always have to lug it around?"

"I don't know. I'm used to it. I didn't have it before you. Before I met you, Gerald."

"I'm not him anymore."

"How can that be?"

"It just is."

The popping came to a close, with just a few singular pops. I poured the contents of the pot into a large ceramic mixing bowl, sprinkled sea salt and then some nutritional yeast on top. I poured some yeast into Humphrey's bowl. He licked it up eagerly.

"What the hell is that?" Shirley asked tartly.

"Nutritional yeast."

"Oh yes. I remember. You always put that on popcorn. Annoyed the hell out of me."

"I did?"

"Yes. You see. You're still the same person."

"No, I'm not. I know that. A lot of people have a hankering for nutritional yeast on popcorn."

"Not that many."

"Shirley, what is going to bring you some peace?"

"I won't have peace until I have destroyed your life. Like you destroyed mine."

"How did I destroy your life? It doesn't seem destroyed."

"By killing yourself. By killing yourself with drugs you killed part of me. I felt so guilty for it all. And that filled me with rage. And for what?! You didn't even die."

"Yes I did. And besides. You weren't responsible. Sounds like I was a terrible nihilist who got what was coming."

"Yes. But you were also loving. And I loved you. In fact, if not most then a good chunk of the time, you were kind to me and lavished me with affection. I never knew how much I missed that until you were gone."

"So, I wasn't all bad?"

"That's right. Not all bad. And now it seems you have been reborn, with most of the bad, if not all, from what I can see, gone, and now you are almost completely good. Why does Minh get that? It's not fair. And I won't stand for it."

"What are you going to do?"

"You'll see."

CHAPTER 50

◆

I carried the large ceramic Crate and Barrel bowl of popcorn out to the porch. Humphrey in stride and Shirley behind me with smaller bowls. I placed the popcorn on the low teak table and went back to my spot, leaning against the banister. Shirley put down the bowls with a drop and sat back down next to Minh who was nursing Thanh. Everybody stared at the bowl of popcorn as if it were some kind of magic orb. The moment was completely still. No wind blowing the leaves on the trees. No traffic on the street. Nobody moving or speaking. Thanh stopped nursing. I counted the seconds. Two hundred and twenty-two, and then Towson sneezed. Dorothy got up and filled a bowl with popcorn and sat back down. Towson followed Dorothy's lead and we were in motion again.

"This is so good. I love nutritional yeast on popcorn," Towson said exuberantly, almost as if ze were drunk.

"Jesus," Shirley muttered under her breath.

Minh turned to Shirley. "Will you get me a bowl please?"

Shirley, a bit taken aback by this request, which was pleasant and even affectionate, did as she was asked.

I filled a bowl for myself. I looked at Minh and daintily put a single piece of popcorn in my mouth. This made Minh smile because she would often tease me about how I liked to shove big handfuls of popcorn in my mouth, getting the mustard-yellow nutritional yeast flakes all over the front of my shirt.

"I was just telling your husband that I was going to destroy his life, in the way that he had destroyed mine. Not the same way. But destroy it nevertheless."

"Oh really. How are you going to do that? Are you going to try to set our house on fire again? Shirley, what is it that you are after? I'm just not sure of your motive. Is it revenge for things that happened a long time ago?"

"Not so long ago?"

"A lifetime ago."

"Whose lifetime?"

"Dorothy's. Geronimo's, mine, even yours."

"Poppycock!"

"Even if I didn't like you, which I do, I don't think that it is a good idea for you to go around committing arson. Not good for anyone."

"I did not try to set your house on fire."

"Fine. The curtains in the kitchen then. Which could have set the house on fire."

"I did not set anything on fire. And even if I had, I am sure that you used fire retardant paint, and so there was no such chance of the house burning down. But like I said before, I did not set your fucking curtains on fire."

"Then how would you explain the fire?"

"I don't know, Minh. I don't have an explanation for it."

"Okay, say you didn't light the fire. How do you plan on destroying Geronimo's and my and Thanh's life? Because we are inexorably linked. As are you, don't you know."

"Nobody is linked to anyone. We are all singular. That whole idea is just a mirage. You'll see. But he is going to pay and I am going to make him pay for his past lives. You see, there will be justice, there will be retribution; you had your nice life, you got to enjoy a few good years, but now that part is over, now comes the part of great struggle, maybe you will rise to the challenge, who knows. Would you stop that baby from staring at me? Because I won't stop, do you hear me? That baby is freaking me out."

Shirley looked at me, her eyes frightened. Then, as if by magnetic pull, she went back to looking at Thanh. Thanh's face was placid, her mouth firmly set and her arms folded in front of her as if she were scolding. It almost seemed as if her eyes were emitting light, bright white light. And I told myself that I was creating that, in my mind, it was an optical illusion, that the glare from the sun reflecting off of something was creating that illusion. I told myself that whether it was an optical illusion or not the baby was asserting control over the situation. And it was ironclad.

"That baby, that baby, she is staring at me, and she is trying to do something to me with her eyes." Shirley stood up, took a few steps backward away from the baby, yet kept her eyes locked on Thanh's. Or the other way around. "Stop! Stop it. I can't take it. I can't take this! It's evil! It's evil! There is evil in me. Oh my god!" And Shirley collapsed and fell to the ground. I rushed over to where she lay and got down on my knees. Dorothy and then Towson got down around her. Dorothy grabbed her hand. "Mom, Mom, are you alright?" Shirley did not move. I lifted her head with cupped hands. I put my ear to her mouth. I could hear her breathe. It sounded like someone pumping a bicycle tire very slowly. "Shirley, can you hear me?" She didn't move. I looked up, and at Minh, who held a phone in her hand. "An ambulance is on its way," she said.

CHAPTER 51

◆

"She was a lousy mom. But come on, what do you expect? I don't mean she wasn't capable, because she was. She was just not very motherly. No affection; at least not until I got to my teens. By then I didn't need it. I had books and movies. But she became more friendly. We got to be pals. She sold the gallery, cashed out, and she needed a friend. If anything, I became the mom, or mom-like. Also, I must say, I really like her, I mean, she is really funny, if you like that kind of caustic wit. She can walk into a room, say something to offend someone, or everyone, there, but then turn it around by making another quip, and crack everyone up. And then all is okay. But mostly she is alone. Doesn't have any friends. Any time she says that she has made a friend or found someone she likes, a man, you can set your watch, because in a week, maybe two, or in the rare instance as long as a month, the whole thing blows up with acrimony and castigations. I feel sorry for her. But, you know, she doesn't feel sorry for herself. I've never seen that. Until now. Now, I think she feels robbed. Robbed in life, robbed of the kind of love, the kind of love she sees in you and Geronimo. She never had that with him, the him of who he was before. Or maybe she did, to a lesser degree, when he wasn't on drugs or consumed with scoring. I don't know. I wasn't there. It's hard for me to picture him like that. Though, I have to admit, I am looking at him a little differently now that I know more of the backstory. I don't love him any less, and I am so grateful that I have found him and that he is my father, I just understand more why she is like she is."

We sat in chairs around the hospital bed that Shirley lay in. Minh, Dorothy, and me. We had been there for hours. Towson was home with Thanh. Dorothy and Minh must have thought I was asleep. The way they were talking. And I did fall asleep for a little while. I felt so tired, so exhausted by everything that had transpired in the last twenty-four hours. At the Paris Theater, watching Minh and me on the screen, watching Minh giving birth to Thanh, reliving all of that. The question and answer session after the screening and how Shirley tried to blow it all up. She hadn't imagined that I would anticipate her moves. I had hired a private investigator before my book came out to find out the status of the case with Shirley's husband, if it was still open. If it was not classified as a homicide. The case was closed. Accidental death. But my private investigator also found out that I had never actually been married to Shirley. The papers were never sent in.

After the Q and A we gave Dorothy and Towson a ride back to their apartment. They wanted to come back to Ditmas with us. Dorothy didn't want to face her mom, even when I told her to have empathy for her, she had had a tough go of it. When Minh and I got home and put Thanh in her crib, we got into bed and started to make love. But before we could get too far Minh asked for me to get her a glass of wine from downstairs. She was a little nervous about making love, feeling self-conscious, which had been the case since Thanh was born. I went downstairs and poured her a glass of Chianti and grabbed a scented candle from the living room, the Fern + Moss one which I knew she loved. I took it to the kitchen, grabbed a pack of matches from the utility drawer, but the candle wouldn't light, it had burned too low, the wick was covered in wax, and so I set it on the ledge of the kitchen sink. Somehow the candle must have reignited, and somehow the curtain must have made contact. Probably from a loose dangling thread. The curtain was made of a vintage farmhouse grain sack. I was remembering all of this as I sat in the chair listening to Dorothy and Minh with my eyes closed.

"She denied lighting the fire. I've never heard her be dishonest, about anything. She is kind of reverent about property, more so than humans. The house that I grew up in, in Pasadena, she loved and took great pride in it. Your house reminds me of it, though they are totally different. That house in Pasadena was designed by Richard Neutra, all flat roof, post and beam Chinese influence, yet the aesthetic is similar. My dad's furniture definitely has a Danish influence. And in both cases it feels like home. Homey. Because it is pretty and uncluttered and there is air. I loved that house and I miss it. It was Mom who encouraged me to come to New York and attend NYU because she knew I wanted to be a filmmaker. Not that there aren't any film schools in Los Angeles; the place is stupid with film schools. I could have gone to UCLA, but she knew that I needed a place that was visually enthralling. She said that I could pick any random corner in New York City, stand there with my camera, and I would get hundreds of exciting visual images, and film is about images. The text is secondary. That's what she told me. And she is right."

"You're a very gifted filmmaker and artist, she is partly responsible for that and wholly responsible for raising you."

"Look at her, she looks like an angel asleep like that. Minh, you said that you liked her."

"I did. I do. She's a character. A real trickster."

"Yeah, that she is. Setting your house on fire though. That's not her."

"The way she was talking at the house—she was being quite threatening."

I opened my eyes and sat up. "Shirley didn't set the curtains on fire. I did."

Dorothy and Minh looked at me in astonishment. "But why? Why did you do that?" Dorothy implored.

"By accident. And quite stupidly. I can't believe that I blocked it out of my mind. I lit a candle before going upstairs. It didn't ignite because of how low the wick sat in the wax and so I set it on the edge of the sink, not in the sink because there were dishes still there. I know there were loose strands of thread from the vintage sack curtain. The candle must have produced a flame and then a thread caught that."

"How could you have forgotten?" Minh asked sharply.

Taken aback by her tone, I shot back defensively, "Because, it didn't seem possible, because there was so much going on that night, because I was thinking about pleasing you."

"What?"

"I was thinking not about the candle that didn't light, but about getting back to you."

"Oh, Geronimo. How careless. And to let Shirley take the blame."

"I didn't mean for that to happen."

Shirley groaned. Dorothy got up and went to her side. "Mom? How are you feeling?"

Shirley opened her eyes. "What happened to me?"

"Vasovagal syncope. Your blood pressure got really low because you were dehydrated, and hadn't eaten for a long time, and standing so suddenly, you fainted."

"Because of that baby's eyes."

I got up out of my chair and went over to the side of the bed. "Shirley, I need to confess something to you."

"You killed Antonio?"

"No. I don't think so. But I did start the fire. Accidentally."

"I know. I heard your confession just now. Poppycock. You know, you have a tendency to conveniently 'not remember' things that happened. Things that won't look good for you."

"Seems that way," I admitted.

"Now hold on," Minh interjected. "Let's not draw broad conclusions. Geronimo admitted what happened."

"Don't make excuses for him. He hasn't 'come clean' about his past. Before his near-death or death experience, whatever."

"I'm not making excuses, Shirley. But I know this man, and he is good."

"I'm not saying that he is not fundamentally good. I'm just saying that men fuck up and then plead either being unaware of destructive intent, or claim it never happened."

"Mom, maybe you're right to a certain degree, but can't we just move on? Leave things in the past and find a peaceful way forward?" Dorothy extended her hand to Shirley who clasped it.

"Yes, that's what I have planned to do. I have already set the wheels in motion."

"What do you mean, Shirley?" Minh asked.

"I told you there would be retribution. Maybe that is an overstatement. Or maybe that is an understatement. Either way you two are not the only writers in this twisted family. I have written a memoir which is due to be released by Doubleday shortly. It's actually a perfectly timed companion piece to your novel *Coming Clean*, Geronimo, only it fills in the blanks where yours leaves off, and I must say it doesn't paint a pretty picture. It's called *Feeling Dirty*."

CHAPTER 52

◆

Shirley's book came out and all hell broke loose. Overnight I was dropped by my publisher and simultaneously became the poster boy for "The Survivors," an organization of mostly white men kicking back against the "illuminated" movement. In Shirley's book *Feeling Dirty*, she made accusations that I had been verbally and emotionally abusive. And she brought up the slapping incident, glossing over her coldcocking me. I was an arrogant and narcissistic man, part of the entitled patriarchy and—to The Survivors—a victim and a hero.

For Minh and myself it felt like a serious interruption to our idyllic life. The landline had to be disconnected. I was receiving constant requests for interviews to comment on Shirley's memoir. I was tempted but Minh talked me out of it. She cryptically said I should wait until I had more information. But in reality I had no comment. Shirley's recollection of the years before I died had the air of truth. And her writing was pithy and her prose crisp, like how she spoke. Her Welsh upbringing came through in her style, which rang like a more contemporary version of Dylan Thomas. And it was hilarious, which meant it sold like hotcakes.

Minh's show on Netflix, *Mai - Superhero Supergirl*, was also a hit. Young people were going crazy over it, and she was contracted for another season. There were suggestions that she change the name to *Mai - Super Hero Super Ze*. An idea she entertained—after all, Mai had no sexual orientation, her character's sexuality was purely neutral. Except that she was a girl, at least in Minh's conception. Even Minh had to admit that if the character didn't identify as such then she or ze could be anything to anyone. It didn't really matter much as she saw it. Yet, now that we had the first ze president, the issue had become that much more prominent, and more and more people were going that way. Minh started developing the idea for another story about a Ze Super Hero Super Poet—Luu, whose magical powers were to create poems that altered people's perceptions in a positive way. When people were stuck in a tough situation, or perhaps sad because of an illness or the loss of a loved one, or an evildoer about to do evil, this superhero would arrive out of nowhere and with a poem guide the person in trouble to a peaceful and enlightened place.

"I think you should do it," Minh told me as we lay in bed on a cold morning in early December.

"Do what?" I replied while stretching my arms toward the ceiling and making a low guttural sound with my voice.

"Respond."

"Respond?"

"To *Feeling Dirty*."

"Yeah?"

"Yeah. But first you should go to the Blank Institute and spend time in the memory chamber, to try to see what you can recollect."

"Blank Institute? Oh yes, the Blank Institute; because I am drawing a blank? What is it—some kind of clinic for people with Alzheimer's?"

"There are more people with your kind of condition than you know."

"People who died and forgot their previous life?" I said, a little sarcastically. And immediately felt bad about my tone. "Well, I don't want to do it."

"Geronimo, the time has come for you to really confront your past. Confront yourself."

"Really?"

"Yes."

"I suppose that you're right. But one thing you know about

me is that I am a coward."

"Oh, quite the contrary. I think you are the bravest man that I have ever known."

"Oh Minh. Your love sustains me."

"Your love sustains me, too. And will sustain me when I have to go to Los Angeles next week for discussions with the studio. They want me to join the executive board for programming."

"What? That's a real departure for you. I mean, you're an artist, a writer."

"I am many things."

"Yes, I know."

"But what about me and the baby?"

"It will just be for a week or so. She is weaned and you have Towson and Dorothy to help."

"I guess. Okay."

"And I think that you will be more settled after your therapy."

"What therapy?"

"The memory chamber. The Blank Institute. You forgot already! I made an appointment for you. Four consecutive days. Tuesday to Friday. Next week. It's an early birthday gift."

"I don't even know when my birthday is."

"It's August 9th. Remember? The detective found it."

"Oh yes. I need coffee."

Minh left for Los Angeles on Monday. On Tuesday I began my therapy at the Blank Institute. Coincidentally the institute was only about ten blocks from our house, over in Kensington. I could walk there. It was a warm morning, so sunny that I wore sunglasses. As I strolled along I thought to myself how funny all of it was, all of it, my life and pre-life. And now I was walking to a place called the Blank Institute, to go into a memory chamber to recollect what had happened to me before I died, before I was twenty-two. It was bound to be mostly not good. Still, I had to do it. I had to do it because Minh said I had to do it. And she was always right. Even though she hated when I said it.

A simple building with the number 50 printed in bold Helvetica font on a white door. 50 Fenimore Street. I turned the large brass knob in the middle of the door and it slowly opened. I walked into a white room; the door closed behind me. There was a window on the far wall which I went to. On the counter below the window was a computer tablet. At the top of the tablet was my name, Geronimo Vang, and beneath that were the words: Introductory Questionnaire. A short list of four questions:

1)   What is your first memory?
2)   What did you have for breakfast?
3)   What was the last thing that you remember dreaming?
4)   What would you rather be: a bird or a fish?

1) My first memory is picking kiwis. Hunched over for hours in the Central California sun. Wearing oversized dungarees, boots, a white T-shirt, and a San Francisco Giants baseball cap. Picking kiwis is not fun, because of the height of the kiwi tree; you have to be slightly bent over to get to them, and after hours of picking your back hurts like hell.

2) I had a cup of coffee and a chocolate chip cookie that Dorothy had brought me for breakfast. She smiled expectantly, even proudly. She was excited for the day, for me.

3) I dreamt the night before that we got another puppy, a cute black-and-white Jack Russell. The pup had trouble walking because the floor to our house was missing. We all had no problem walking without a floor. Minh was there, and Dorothy and Thanh, who was not walking but crawling. There was no floor, just air. But the new puppy kept stumbling because of it. And I said to myself, "This is very frustrating." Minh said, "Don't worry, it's only a dream." And then I woke up.

4) I would much rather be a bird, and fly above all of this, fly in the air and look down, look down from afar, at the city and the neighborhoods and then fly to our house and land on the banister of our porch and look at my loved ones. And then fly up and away.

After I finished with the questions the tablet flashed: GO THROUGH THE BLUE DOOR. And indeed there was a blue door at the end of the room. I went through it. The memory chamber truly was not what you might have imagined. It was just a small room with a bed. The room was painted a creamy white, like whipping cream, and the bed was a single with two white fluffy pillows and a simple blue quilt. I sat down on the bed. I looked around the room. Nothing to see. My feet felt a little sore. Not like I had walked a great distance. Still I felt like liberating them, and so I took off my Padror Noir shoes. And then the red argyle socks. I stretched my legs and wiggled my toes. Thought I heard whispers. Looked around. Nothing. I lay back on the bed, put my hands clasped behind my head. I was not waiting for someone to enter. I was not waiting for a therapist. I already knew that there was no therapist. I hadn't read anything about the Blank Institute. I wanted to go in without any preconceptions, but as I had yet to see a person it felt like a foregone conclusion that there were no humans in the building. There was a side table by the bed and on the side table was a lamp made out of a clarinet. The light turned off, and then a strobe light, it was coming from somewhere, though I could not determine its source, it alternated slowly and quickly. For some reason this made me laugh. Really? This was it? This was the therapy? This was what was going to get me to that place where all the memories came flooding back. The strobe was making me nauseous. Yet all I had to do to shut out the strobing light was close my eyes. I did that.

And I slept, and I dreamt, and I saw my life. Not just my life but many lives, going backward and then forward. It was as if my cells could talk, tell a story, as if my cells were re-personified. And given face and body and tasks. I was inside of them and outside of them, first and third person. Cro-Magnon, picking flowers, making something to eat out of flowers, using a wooden bowl and stone, eating with others, laying on the ground, making love, fucking, not like a beast but like a timid soul. I am man, I am woman, I am child, I am elderly, and I die, and what flashes before me is many lives, and a cascading tapestry of light. And there is fear, overwhelming fear, and then there is acceptance. And then there is silence. And then I open my eyes and the strobe has ceased, and six hours have passed. And I am so terribly hungry.

Each day, in the memory chamber, I progress in time, through the centuries, through the many physical embodiments of my shared soul. Each day is more dense with it, more fascinating. I am so exhausted and hungry and thirsty when I get home I can barely speak. Dorothy asks me how it went and I just smile. And she smiles back. Minh calls and she tells me about her day because she knows that I can barely speak. And when I go to bed I don't put Thanh in her crib, she sleeps with me. This makes her very happy. She smiles. Her eyes alight. She searches my eyes for something, something that confuses her. And then she finds it, and in the most gentle way she touches my arm and says, "Dada." And when I wake in the morning it is as if all the dreams from the previous night are stored in a microchip.

On the last day at the institute I am me. The me I was before I died. Red hair, lanky, gruff. Playing in the dirt of the desert, in the sand of dry land. My mother is cooking dinner, she makes enchiladas, my father drinks from a bottle; says he is going to the city. Says he has written poems and he is going somewhere to read them. My mother says, "Poems are imaginary gardens with real toads in them." At bedtime she reads from e. e. cummings, from Marianne Moore, from the Bible. We say prayers and she kisses me good night. And I am a young man. And I am in school. And I feel untouchable. And I want to fuck any of the beautiful young women in my classes. And I fantasize about it. But when I finally have my chance, I don't know how to. It is embarrassing. But only a blip.

I am self-obsessed. Self-possessed. And I find drink, and a drug that makes me feel like a satellite. And it annoys me that I am this way. I let a beard grow. Want to cover my face. But then I meet a woman. And she cuts me to the quick. She is lacerating with her wit. And I fall in love, or think it's love. But I don't change, though I want to. More than want to, will to. But it's no good. Just can't. She says it's because I don't love her and that the only person I love is myself. I say, "Poppycock!"

She is rich, richer than me, who has nothing, except an education, and a love of books and a desire to write. But I don't write. Or I barely write. I get a job at a newspaper, but that is rote. She thinks I've changed. And we get married. Pretty party. Lots of her friends, who look at me like I am a freak. Which I am. Or feel like. She thinks I've changed. But secretly she only hopes I've changed, she knows I haven't. We fight with words, and once when I am in a drug stupor, she slugs me across the face. I turn, there's her face, radiant with anger, I smile, smile and gently touch her cheek. We make love and the baby is conceived.

The baby changes everything for me. I now have a purpose. But that doesn't last long. And I am back. Back to drugs and to being a "bloody nihilist," as she says. And she takes the baby and leaves me for another man. For Antonio. And I descend. Into drugs and confusion and inner chaos. On the night before I die I go around to her gallery. I look through the window. There is Antonio. Way up on a ladder. He looks so magnificent, so assured with each movement of a large brush. He paints on an extraordinarily big canvas, so large that he has to use a double extension ladder to reach the top. Music plays, opera: *Lucia Di Lammermoor*. The soprano laments, wails, almost a cappella: she has seen the ghost of a girl killed in the very same spot she stands; the apparition is a warning that she must give up her love. Antonio cries, and even though the wall muffles the sound of the diva, her voice moves me profoundly, moves me to tears. I cry because my soul is shattered, because I know that I am a shell, a disgrace to humanity, but that it is possible to redeem myself. And all at once I wail, I howl like a wounded animal. Antonio looks up abruptly at the sound of my guttural cry, he is in shock, dispersed from his reverie, and he loses balance and falls from the ladder, landing headfirst on the concrete floor. And I know he is dead.

CHAPTER 53

◆

My first interview was on the Forrest Burleson show. Forrest was not looking good. His hair dyed Cadillac black and his face stretched back like a still picture of an astronaut during g-force. But his eyes were still the same, same malignant intent. I am not sure what he had heard or read about me and what he was expecting, but I don't think it went as planned.

FORREST: Geronimo. Can I call you that, or would you prefer Gerald?

MYSELF: Geronimo, please, but either is fine. I was once called Gerald, though I have no recollection of that.

FORREST: Exactly. Your former self is being held up to contemporary standards. Not just held up but persecuted. How does that feel?

MYSELF: Great!

FORREST: Great because you are up for the fight, because you can bear witness to how far we have descended in these witch hunts. After all, simply because it was alleged that you were once a bit of a cad, and maybe slapped a lady in the heat of a marital squabble, suddenly your whole life is turned upside down. Your career derailed. And now you have been embraced by The Survivors, a group of which I am a member, proudly. It is only by the grace of God that I am one of the survivors. And I must say, we still don't know what caused the terrible plague that devastated the white male community.

MYSELF: Yes we do. Beer and red meat.

FORREST: That's what we are being told.

MYSELF: By the scientific community. I believe in science.

FORREST: So do I, but . . .

MYSELF: I know what you are getting at, but let's cut to the chase. I am not a victim, if my career has been "derailed," as you say, then my goodness, it is by my own doing. I am not a victim, I am the perpetrator. I am one of the ones who have embraced and asserted my dominance in all the different ways afforded me, but now, because of the events of the last few years, that has changed. And I am just one of the many who has to start over, again. Starting over again is not so bad, in fact it is a blessing. And Forrest, you are never too old to start over . . .

FORREST: Start over! But . . .

MYSELF: Yes, that's right. Let's start over. Let's throw out un-useful behavior and language and replace it with that which empowers people. Let's face it, the tables have turned, and we are in the minority; we are in the minority when it comes to our sex and to our status, so let's embrace humility. Why? Because not only will it make for a more cohesive society, it will actually make our own lives better.

FORREST: Yes but . . .

MYSELF: Yes but what? The economy is in the best shape in a hundred years, dire poverty has pretty much been eliminated, the climate has stabilized, and there are fewer and fewer catastrophic environmental events. Crime is nil, and this all happened since men have lost power. It's been an extraordinary turn of events. And I for one am only grateful for it, and look forward to a world where both of my daughters and people of every kind of orientation can thrive in ways that the past has never afforded them. If I lost a publisher, who cares. Who fucking cares! Besides, I'm in between ideas anyway. Now, that's all I wanted to say.

I took off my microphone and left.

When I got home, I was greeted at the door by Dorothy, who threw her one free arm around me; her other arm held Thanh, who reached up, touched my face, and said, "Dada." My phone buzzed. I took it from my pocket. It was Minh, who was still in LA. Her face was radiant, filled with ebullient expression and deep affection. She said, "Darling. I'm so proud of you." And I knew that all of this was part of living memory, a fulfillment of desire, and a manifestation of a kind of life I once only dreamt of.